OMNIVM
LVX
CIVIVM
MDCCCLII
MDCCC
LXXVIII

Never Paint a Stranger

Never Paint a Stranger

Patricia Shaw

A TOM DOHERTY ASSOCIATES BOOK
NEW YORK

This is a work of fiction. All the characters and events portrayed in this book are fictitious, and any resemblance to real people or events is purely coincidental.

NEVER PAINT A STRANGER

A TOR BOOK
Published by Tom Doherty Associates, Inc.
49 West 24 Street
New York, NY 10010

First edition: May 1989
0 9 8 7 6 5 4 3 2 1

To family and friends who were patient, and thought I could do it, and, not least, for the one who thought I couldn't.

P·R·O·L·O·G·U·E

THE gardens of Lura Livorna were never prettier than in September, 1916. If Imperial Russia writhed in death throes, you'd never know it from the vivid faces of the autumn dahlias. Banks of chrysanthemums—orange, red, pale amber—were set off by tall drifts of purple asters. Winding stone paths were swept clean of debris. A reflecting pool rippled scarlet and gold with images of overhanging trees.

Oblivious of the splendor, Ilse Bonnard paced inside an English pavilion of the style made popular by Catherine the Great. Eight long strides, whirl, eight strides again. Gusting breezes caught her skirt, she captured the billowy folds and smoothed them compulsively.

Leaves rustled, a dead twig snapped. The screech of a peahen pursued by a randy cock shattered the air. Shrieks from the tame fowl were commonplace, but Ilse shrank against an ivied stone column and stifled a wail of her own.

Fool, fool. It was a bird, a stupid, silly bird. Pull yourself together. You can't help Lisanne if you're a quivering, hysterical mass.

She sat on a Chippendale bench. Think. Plan. That's what she had to do.

Her nostrils flared at the scent of pungent smoke. Had it come already? The sweet, cloying fetor of burning human flesh?

No. Her body sagged. Leaves from the linden trees smoldered where they had been gathered and burned in the chill of early morning. Only linden smoke, but Ilse pictured black, sooty eruptions from the maws of belching cannons, heard the jangle of harness and the rumble of caissons. Revolution would come to Lura Livorna. It would howl into the countryside, as inevitable as the harsh reality of Russian winter.

She was a guest in the home of her childhood friend, the Grand Duchess Lisanne Nicholaevich. Shivering in the English pavilion, she remembered the night before. Lisanne's husband, Grand Duke Peter Nicholaevich, had come home.

His appearance had been a happy surprise for Lisanne. "Petra," as he was called by friends and family, had been in the thick of battle on the German front for months. His infrequent letters, borne by military courier, told of outnumbered Russian forces brutally decimated by the army of Kaiser Wilhelm. Petra was a trusted commander, only the necessity of escorting Tsar Nicholas himself from the battlefield to the Winter Palace had made this brief visit possible.

The news he brought was terrifying. He told the women of grim events in Petrograd; of anger, confusion, resentment gushing through the streets with the stench of sour wine and eddying about the walls of the Winter Palace, where the royal family lived in a state of near siege.

While the Tsar was at the battlefront Tsarina Alexandra ruled Russia. Everyone but Nicholas knew Alexandra was controlled by the hypnotic renegade monk, Rasputin.

Profligate, lecherous, called a fiend from hell by orthodox churchmen, Rasputin held absolute power over the Tsarina, for one reason. He alone could stop the terrifying attacks of hemophilia that afflicted her only son, the little Tsarevitch.

In a mad dance orchestrated by the insane monk, Alexandra caused government officials to rise and fall like puppets in a Punch and Judy show. Talk of assassination and the inevitability of revolution was as common as discussion of the weather, or news from the front.

Stunned by the situation as Petra explained it, Ilse had gone to her room early, giving husband and wife a chance to be alone. She had not seen them again until the noon meal today, when she had been confronted with a fervent plea. They wanted her to go home to Switzerland at once, taking their five-year-old daughter, Madeleine, to the safety of Basel.

"I already have your papers, Ilse. Madie is identified as your child, born in Russia. An old friend from Geneva is traveling home with his wife, they will come for you tonight. You are citizens of a neutral country, you should have no trouble getting through."

"You must do it, Ilse," Lisanne joined in. "I have to know Madie's safe. Petra wanted to send her to America with Demi, but I couldn't allow it, I just couldn't. So far away. She loves you, she'll be happy in Switzerland. Say you will."

"But you and Petra . . . I need time to think," Ilse had blurted. That was when she left the table without excusing herself and ran out into the garden.

Freshening wind plucked at her skirt again, exposing a flannel petticoat. She pulled the layers of fabric close against her body and tucked the fullness under her legs.

Why wouldn't they face what seemed so clear? The old ways were dead. Lisanne and Petra had to leave Lura Livorna and never look back, or be victims of the blood lust of beautiful, savage Russia.

"Ilse? Are you out there? Where are you?" The soft, familiar voice intruded, bittersweet as the linden smoke.

She didn't answer. Lisanne found her anyway.

"Come inside, please. It's cold, there's a storm brewing. We haven't much time, Ilse. You have to pack."

Ilse touched the chair beside her. "In a minute. Sit down, I have something to say."

Lisanne pulled a crimson dahlia head, its petals fell one by one from her pale fingers and were swept away by the wind. She perched on the seat's edge.

"Ilse, please don't let's quarrel, not now." Her face was pinched inside its frame of wild, dark curls. Ugly shadows ringed gray eyes soft as a dove's breast. She looked back toward the house and plucked at her hair with nervous, random gestures.

An affectionate smile softened the angular planes of Ilse's face. "Don't quarrel, Ilse," she mimicked. "How many times have I heard that?"

The smile disappeared. "It won't work this time, I'll say my piece. You've got to get out of here, Lisanne. Wake up, you're living in a make-believe world. Russia is a crazed wolf who will once again devour her children."

Lisanne's face was turned away, toward the haunting beauty of the house. "It's not that bad. People will come to their senses and realize what a great man the Tsar is.

"I could throttle that bitch of a Tsarina, though. It's all her fault, this trouble with the peasants. Hers and that filthy 'holy man' who has her hypnotized. As if the Tsar didn't have his hands full, fighting the German invasion!"

Lisanne leaned forward to emphasize her words. "Alexandra's gone completely mad. Did I tell you her sister Elizabeth left the monastery and paid a visit to the Winter Palace? She pled with the Tsarina to banish Rasputin. Alexandra was furious, she ordered Elizabeth to leave! Her own sister. A nun, a saint, sent off like a cur dog kicked away from the dinner table."

Ilse shrugged. "What's one more arrogant act?"

The dahlia's nude stalk fell from Lisanne's fingers. "It'll be better now Tsar Nicholas is home. He'll see how bad the situation is, and take action."

"He won't, he's never crossed her before. Why do you suppose they call him the 'Bloodless Mannequin'? She'll keep on running things from her precious mauve boudoir, until someone carries her off and hacks her to pieces."

Lisanne shuddered. "Don't talk like that.

"It is a shame, though, that Petra wasn't born heir to the throne, instead of his cousin Nicholas. Petra's a natural leader, he'd be a magnificent tsar. If only . . ."

Ilse flung a hand out in irritation. "If, if. He couldn't have married you, if he were tsar. That's beside the point, Lisanne. Petra is the Tsar's cousin; if the Bolsheviks come to Lura Livorna you'll be butchered like the lambs you are. You have no choice but to come to Switzerland with me. Now. Today."

A high, unnatural laugh burst from Lisanne's lips. "How silly! That rabble, here? As soon as this German thing is finished our loyalist armies will . . . besides, we couldn't possibly go. What about Lura Livorna? Our house in Petrograd? My husband refuses to become an expatriate and live in Paris or New York, the way some of his family has. Never, Ilse. Russia is our home."

"If you stay here you haven't a chance. Give a thought to Demi and Madie, do you want them to be orphans?"

Lisanne covered her ears with unsteady palms. Her head dropped.

As minutes passed, Ilse began to hope her brutal words had been worth the pain it caused to utter them.

She was wrong. Lisanne stood, assumed the dignity of a Grand Duchess. "I won't listen to this. If you don't want to take Madeleine until things are settled—"

Ilse recognized defeat. "I'll take Madie, of course. Let's go inside and pack."

• • •

Lisanne stood looking down at her sleeping daughter. Night shadowed the room, the child's face seemed flushed in the light of a bedside candle. Strands of dark hair fanned over her satin pillow. She was already dressed to travel in navy merino wool with sailor collar and matching long stockings. Black kidskin boots stood at attention on the floor.

"She's such an observant little girl, Ilse. She'll sense something's wrong, I know she will."

Ilse commanded Lisanne away from the bed with an emphatic gesture. "Shhh, you'll wake her.

"She's not going to sense a thing if we all keep our heads. She believes what you told her. A short holiday in Switzerland with Tante Ilse. You're her mother, why would she doubt you?"

Tears glistened in Lisanne's eyes. "You're right. My baby trusts me, I've never lied to her before. Ah, God, Ilse, I hate this!"

"It can't be helped. It's me she'll blame when I don't bring her back. She won't be angry with you."

Ilse walked to an open wardrobe trunk. She picked up three tucked batiste petticoats, stuffed them in, then pushed the trunk shut and looked at her locket watch. "It's nine. Petra will come for Madie and me in a few minutes."

Lisanne felt a sudden urge to commit her friend to memory: the strong, handsome planes of her square face, with its frame of sorrel hair that parted in the middle and looped back into a glossy knot at the base of her skull. The tall, spare body that seemed always to be in motion. So dear, so familiar, a part of her youth. Would she ever see Ilse again?

Lisanne's scrutiny seemed to make Ilse uneasy. She blurted out inanities, her voice too loud in the silent room. "Madeleine's clothes and mine in one trunk. Petra won't believe it. Neither do I, really. Why, do you remember . . ." Her face crumpled. She clutched Lisanne's arm.

"Change your mind. Come with us, you and Petra. You must. The hell with Russia, the Romanovs, Lura Livorna. My family loves you like their own, you know that. They'd be so happy to have you home again. Then, when everything's safe, you can . . ." her voice trailed off.

Lisanne pulled away and walked to a tall armoire.

"A visit to the peace and sanity of Basel. Heaven on earth. Oh, Ilse, you tempt me, but it's impossible. I will not go without Petra, and he won't even consider it.

"Give my love to Madame and Monsieur, though, and your brother. Make them understand how much it means to me, knowing Madie will be in your care. Perhaps someday Petra and I can make it up to all of you. . . ."

She opened the armoire's double doors and took out an Oriental box of carved teak. She raised the lid, releasing the pungent scent of camphor wood.

"Do me a favor and get some candles, will you, Ilse? Half of these are gutted, and we have no oil for the lamps. I want the house ablaze with light; we don't have to slink around inside our own walls, yet."

Seeming to welcome an excuse for action, Ilse left.

Lisanne moved swiftly. She took a rectangular object from the armoire, wrapped it in bright, embroidered silk, and put it in the box, which she then carried to a writing table.

A small leather bag appeared from the pocket of her dressing gown, she opened it and spilled the contents onto her palm. Rainbow prisms splashed across the wall. Satisfied, she refilled the bag and tucked it into a corner of the teak box, beside the silk-wrapped object. She picked up paper and pen and began to write.

Ilse returned with an armload of candles. When fresh tapers were lit she joined Lisanne at the desk, looking over her shoulder.

"What are you doing?"

"I want you to take something with you. For Madeleine." Lisanne finished writing, folded the paper into its envelope, and reached for a stick of sealing wax, a candle, and a brass seal.

"A letter for a five-year-old?" Ilse asked.

"A letter and some things you can sell."

Ilse frowned. "What are you talking about, things I can sell? We'll take care of Madie. She won't need money."

Lisanne touched her friend's hand. "Don't be insulted. I'm

thinking about the future. In case Petra and I aren't here . . . you understand. I won't have her launched into society penniless, to look for a husband."

"Like you were? You didn't do badly."

Lisanne made an impatient gesture. "That was different. You know what I'm talking about, don't cloud the issue."

Ilse strode to a window and jerked the heavy draperies open. Over her shoulder Lisanne could see rain mixed with sleet pelt the glass. Lightning flashed, the English pavilion loomed like a stage set at the opera.

"The whole situation is monstrous," Ilse said, her voice bleak with impotent anger.

Lisanne dropped a blob of wax onto the envelope and pressed the seal into it. She hadn't noticed before how much the russet wax looked like dried blood.

There was a photograph lying on the table, a sepia print of a man, a woman, two children, and a spaniel. She picked it up. Last summer in the garden, just before Demi left. Madie should have it, Lisanne decided. So she wouldn't forget her family.

"I do believe things will be as they were, Ilse. For now, though, it will ease my mind to send this with her."

She closed the box and held the stick of wax near the candle flame again. When it softened she began applying wax to the seam between box and lid.

"Please yourself." Ilse left the window to watch Lisanne finish the job.

"You're being mysterious. What's in there besides the letter?"

"I don't want you to know. Put it in the bottom of your trunk and forget you have it. If you're stopped and your baggage is searched, say a friend took advantage of your kindness, and asked you to deliver a gift to relatives in Switzerland."

Before Ilse could reply Petra came into the room. As always, the sight of him quickened Lisanne's pulse. His tall, muscular body and chiselled face could have stepped from the pages of a romantic epic. He wore the black boots and blue uniform of a regimental commander, with epaulets and a bandoleer.

He kissed Lisanne hastily and turned to Ilse. "Are you ready? Don't forget, you are a governess returning home. Madie is your child, born in Russia."

Ilse raised an eyebrow. "I hope no one questions me about the father."

Petra ignored the poor attempt at wit. "Do you think you can carry it off? What if Madie cries for her mother?"

"She won't, Petra. Lisanne explained I'm taking her on holiday, and we're going to play-pretend I'm her mama. She's a bright child who loves a good game. She'll be fine."

A new fear gripped Lisanne. She clutched her husband's arm. "Love, I've been so concerned with getting Madie and Ilse ready to leave . . . What if the Bolsheviks stop them, or the Germans? Maybe they'd be better off here, after all."

Petra pulled her against his chest, stroked her hair. "No, my darling, they wouldn't." His arms tightened around her. "I only wish you would go with them."

Lisanne shook her head with violence. "Never. I'm going to be right here at Lura Livorna, waiting for you to come home."

Petra kissed the top of her head and released her, then walked to the bed and knelt beside his daughter. Lisanne followed.

• • •

Ilse turned her back on the family. She picked up the carved teak box and examined it with curiosity. It was unlike Lisanne to be secretive. She shrugged and found a spot for it among her things, then made a long business of closing and locking the trunk.

She heard whimpers as the parents woke their sleeping child, and the loving murmurs with which they comforted her.

Thunder rumbled.

O·N·E

HANNA Anders lay suspended in the amorphous world between waking and sleeping, where every magical thing is possible. The sun was warm. Voluptuous breezes played across her body and teased her nostrils with sensuous fragrances of the ancient island. Mundane problems, out of harmony with the sun and the sea, shrank into a black dot on her mental horizon. The dot wavered, ceased to exist.

"Hanna, why are you leaving?"

Damn. She tried to shut out the question.

"Hanna?"

No use, he wouldn't be ignored. Hanna frowned, her long, golden body rippled into a sitting position. Christian began to brush at the fine film of sand that clung to her shoulders.

"I wouldn't have come to Ibiza if you hadn't said there were ghosts, Christian."

Now he was trickling a stream of sparkling crystals across her toes. He looked up, his lips curved in a grin. Hanna responded with one of her own. He had, she knew, the kind of looks few women could resist; hair the color of pale, hand-churned butter, tanned skin, eyes of marine blue that echoed the water of a shaded Ibizan cove.

"That's not true," he challenged. "You had to meet Malika. I'll bet you came to Europe just to see the man you threw over, and the woman he married."

"Don't be silly, I've had this trip in mind for years."

She trickled sand herself, aiming at the minuscule gap between muscular back and bikini trunks. "I was curious about Malika, I won't deny that. Then you wrote about the ghosts and I was hooked. You tricked me, admit it. So far all I've seen are whitewashed houses, sand, pine trees, and acres of naked flesh toasted to perfection."

Christian laughed. "You can't disapprove of bare, tanned skin. You're displaying a lot of it."

Hanna pulled at the top of her bikini. "I had to buy this. The suit I brought from Denver would have given your Ibizan neighbors something to laugh about for years."

"That demure? I'd forgotten how self-conscious you are about your body. How tall are you; five-ten, five-eleven? Surely not six feet."

"That has nothing to do with it," she lied.

He caught a strand of her long hair and wound it around his hand. "You're gorgeous, Hanna. I remember I used to say your hair reflected all the colors of the sunset. Terrible lovesick drivel."

"I didn't think it was drivel. We were art students, we thought in terms of color. I still do."

Shading her eyes with splayed fingers, she looked back across the beach. Christian's house seemed to float, a shimmering mirage on the cliff-side.

"Shouldn't we start home? Malika will be back from Santa Eulalia. She promised to take me to the airport and help with reservations."

Christian picked up her sunglasses, blew sand off the lenses, and gave them to her.

"You haven't changed. Who keeps track of your possessions now?"

"Everyone changes, Christian. I do all right by myself. For the last six months I've ranged over Italy and Spain like a gypsy, carrying my painting gear. I haven't lost a thing."

"Which takes us back to my original question. You've been on the continent all this time without any urgency about visiting Switzerland, so why the sudden rush? You meant to stay with us six weeks; you've barely been two, and you can't wait to get away. Don't you like Malika? Or have you finally recognized the mad passion you have for me? Afraid you'll disgrace yourself?"

Christian's tone was light, but Hanna knew the question was serious. She answered slowly, feeling her way. "You and I were very close at one time. It wasn't enough, Christian. I sensed something . . . some kind of instability in you"—she put out a flat palm as he started to protest—"or in me, that kept me from throwing caution to the winds and running off to Ibiza with you. Maybe I didn't love you enough, maybe I couldn't believe you loved me."

She made a dismissive gesture. "Whatever. That's in the past, it doesn't matter. I love you like a brother, now; and as for Malika, I think she's wonderful. And generous, to welcome your old girlfriend into her home."

Christian made a wry face. "Like a brother. Ouch! Then what is it, Hanna? Why are you going? There has to be a reason."

With a lithe twist of his muscular body he stood and took her hand. They walked to a pair of stone seats tucked away in an almond thicket, where the land began to rise away from the sea.

"Christian, you're one of the few people who know anything about my grandfather."

He frowned, puzzled by the change of subject.

"Your grandfather? Oh, I remember. The mysterious Russian who said you were an heiress. I have to confess I never believed it."

"I know. Fairy tales, told by a lonesome old man to entertain a gullible child."

Christian pointed a strong brown finger. "Wait a minute. He had some connection with Switzerland. Didn't he live there awhile, after his parents shipped him out of Russia?"

"No, that was a sister, his only sibling. My great-grandparents sent Dedushka to the States in 1916; a few months later a family friend took his sister to Basel."

"I remember now, that's where the inheritance business comes in. Didn't you tell me the sister's guardian took something out of Russia, and hid it away for safekeeping? What is it supposed to be? Gold? Jewels?"

Hanna probed rocky soil with the toe of her sandal. "I don't know, he wouldn't tell me. And I only have a vague idea where to start treasure hunting. I don't really expect to find anything, but—here's the crazy part, Christian. I had planned to do some poking around in Basel, but not until spring. I was going to leave here for England in December."

He nodded. "That's what I understood."

"For the past three days, though, I've had the strangest urge to go to Switzerland right now. As if I couldn't get there fast enough."

Christian was morose, his thick golden eyebrows pulled into a scowl of consideration. He drew in an exasperated breath and touched her cheek with the back of his hand.

"I know you're telling the truth, you've never been able to lie. Up to now you haven't been capricious, either."

Hanna smiled. "You were, enough for both of us."

"Don't change the subject, I'm trying to reason this out."

"Christian—"

"Oh, you're going all right, I can see that," he interrupted. "But damn it, Hanna, it doesn't make sense. You're a successful painter. For your age, damned successful. Money's not a problem, anyway." He shook his head.

"Your grandfather's been dead for years. Your father couldn't have put much stock in the story, or he would have checked it out long before you were born."

"Dedushka never told him. He said the inheritance was for me," Hanna said defensively.

"Oooh?" The word was drawn out in beautifully expressed sarcasm.

"So here you are, rushing off to hunt for a problematical treasure as if it were the most important thing in the world. I can't believe it."

Hanna shook her head. "Neither can I. Maybe it's your Ibizan ghosts, after all. A mental manifestation, rather than physical."

He wasn't amused. "I'm concerned about you. Will you keep in touch? Call when you get there?"

"Of course."

His arm came up in a brief gesture of appeal, then dropped.

"We'd better go to the house, you'll want to pack. Malika's friendly with the airline representative, maybe she can get you standby space on this evening's plane for Barcelona. Swissair has a late flight from there to Geneva and you can finish your trip by train."

Hanna got up, the sunglasses falling from her lap.

Christian stooped to retrieve them.

T·W·O

AT 11:47 P.M. Hanna's Swissair flight touched ground on the runway of Cointrin Airport in Geneva. She rode a shuttle bus to town, sharing her seat with a robust, friendly hausfrau who smelled of garlic and perspiration.

The bus unloaded at the midtown train station, Gare Cornavin, and from there she took a taxi to the Hotel Moderne. Riding through colorful, tree-lined streets, she thought of Malika, who had made the reservation for her.

"You should spend the night in Geneva before you go on. I've stayed at the Moderne many times, it's very near Gare Cornavin. Tomorrow ask the concierge for a train schedule, then you can leave at your own convenience."

Hanna remembered bending down to give the exquisite small brunette an awkward hug. "You're very considerate. You must think I'm insane, rushing off like this. Someday I'll come back and explain."

Malika's exotic eyes were sympathetic. She shrugged, conveying "It is of no consequence."

In the cab, Hanna had a flash of insight. What if Malika

thought Christian made a pass at me, and I went tearing off to protect my honor? Poor Christian. What have I done to him?

Remorse was fleeting. Christian could take care of himself.

She checked into the hotel, had a late snack, and curled up in bed to read. When she awoke it was almost noon, the book lay open across her stomach. She yawned, stretched, got up and opened a window. The sun was shining, there was just enough chill in the air for a light jacket over her sweater.

At Gare Cornavin she bought her ticket and found a bench, with almost an hour to kill before train time. She looked around. A man wearing a lynx topcoat intrigued her, pacing up and down with the collar turned up. He must have been roasting.

Has to be an actor, she thought, reaching for her sketch pad. Or an Italian film director? Godfather of an international drug cartel?

She continued speculating as her fingers caught the gesture of the figure in a few strokes, then lingered over his face. Features took shape; short, broad nose, fleshy lips, opaque eyes that were hooded like a cobra's.

Her hand flew back across the paper, putting in heavy lines where she wanted emphasis. The drawing was almost finished when the imperious figure lifted his arm and signalled to catch someone's attention. Two men joined him; thick, brawny types who towered over Fur-coat.

No doubt who's boss, though. He's giving them hell about something.

Fur-coat finished his tirade and stalked off toward the passage leading to the tracks. The hulks followed, looking chastened. Their disappearance reminded Hanna that she was going someplace herself, a quick look at her watch confirmed that she'd almost putzed around too long.

She gathered her things and ran, plagued by clumsiness that was the offspring of haste. The drawing pad with portrait exposed flapped against her leg, held precariously between two fingers.

She caught up with the Cro-Magnon types and their squat boss. Their bulk blocked the passageway. As she squeezed past Fur-coat, he bellowed at her.

Seen your portrait and want it, huh? Sorry, I haven't got time to dicker. Besides, I rather fancy it myself.

Hanna ignored him and ran faster, weaving through knots of people in the track area. A fascist dictator, that was what he looked like. Acted like it, too. Mussolini variety.

She located her train and stepped up into an empty compartment. It was heaven to slump back in the seat and watch anonymous heads move past the window. She surveyed them with idle interest until Fur-coat and his entourage rushed by; that prompted her to lean forward and press her nose against the glass.

Wonder where they're going?

Too late, out of her line of vision. She yawned. Pulling a pillow from the overhead rack, she settled it behind her head, squirmed down to a comfortable slouch, and closed her eyes.

The train pulled out of the station. Its rhythmic swaying was hypnotic; nostalgia took over. Memories of childhood, art school, the years it had taken to make a name for herself as a painter. Old friends reappeared, and the three or four men who had meant something for a while . . . like Christian. She felt alone, forlorn as some old crone whom life had passed by.

Why? It didn't have to be that way. Other artists married and had families, made compromises to exist in the world of normal people. Why hadn't she?

The answer was simple. She loved the freedom of living by herself.

I never found a person who could make me want to give that up.

Have I ever loved anyone? Maybe, but I never trusted a man enough to put my life in his hands.

Except Dedushka. He was different.

She realized she had loved him as only a child can, believed in him with the perfect faith that adults are incapable of feeling.

What if it had all been lies? A family so important he wouldn't whisper the name. A grand inheritance hidden in Switzerland; waiting for time to kill off the players, make retrieval possible. If proof he had been a fake was in Basel, did she really want to know?

It was dark outside when the train whistled her stop. She found an empty baggage cart, loaded her belongings, and pushed it to the locker rental counter. Following established routine, she leased space to stow finished paintings until there were enough accumulated for a shipment to her agent.

She walked to a bank of lockers and found her allotted cubicle. The small key turned with smooth efficiency in the oiled lock. The door swung open. She reached in the cart for her painting carrier.

It wasn't there. She rummaged under the large, rollered suitcase, the portable French easel, a soft canvas supply bag. Not there.

I did not leave it in Geneva. It was here, I put it on top, to go in the locker first.

She retraced her route, dodging a tide of incoming travelers. Her train had departed, there was no sign of the painting carrier along the empty track. A month's work, gone.

She remembered Christian's jibe about her inability to keep track of her belongings. He'd laugh if he could see her now.

Damn bad luck, that's what it was, but there was no use standing around feeling sorry for herself. Maybe the carrier would turn up. She made a report with Lost and Found and told them she'd check back tomorrow.

At the locker she unloaded a canvas bag of spare supplies and opened her portfolio. The drawing pad was inside, her portrait of Fur-coat on the last sheet. She flipped the pages.

"You are a nasty-looking devil," she told him, surprised at the malignant power of the quick sketch. She shoved the pad in the locker and turned away.

The hell with it, she wasn't going to mope around a train station all night. She walked out into the crisp evening. A row of taxis waited at the curb. She hailed one.

T·H·R·E·E

HANNA sat cross-legged on the floor, rooting industriously through her canvas bag and extracting lengths of sized canvas, stretcher strips, and small, wooden shims. Next she brought out a heavy-duty staple gun and huge gripping pliers with fat, serrated teeth. She assembled a set of strips to make an 18- by 24-inch canvas, picked up the staple gun and began shooting sharp metal through fabric and wood.

She had already spent Saturday morning in pajamas, flannel robe, and fuzzy pink slippers, and now had a good start on the afternoon.

The night before she had checked into the Olympia Hotel, had dinner in her room, and gone to bed, but not to sleep. One o'clock, two, three. It was three-thirty when she glared at her black leather travel clock for the last time; at nine she struggled out of bed, tired and grouchy.

She set aside the staple gun and reached for pliers. I'm in Basel, she reminded herself. I moved the moon and stars to get here, so why on earth do I sit alone in a hotel room and stretch canvas?

Ambivalence. After rushing to Switzerland like a fire truck to a conflagration, she wasn't sure what to do next. Pulling pristine linen tight over wooden frames and stapling them together was as good an avoidance tactic as any.

There was no hurry about researching Dedushka's stories, she equivocated. Why not work awhile, get to know the town? Move to another hotel, one that was less expensive and didn't cater to tourists.

She completed five canvases, all she had strips for. Opened the easel box, took out rags, turp, charcoal, brushes, every tube of paint. Dusted the box and wiped it out with a damp cloth. Meticulously cleaned each brush and returned everything to its place in perfect order.

Her stomach rumbled, reminding her she hadn't eaten and it was now midafternoon. Suddenly she was ravenous, a condition that required positive action. She showered, dressed, and headed for the hotel restaurant to devour something.

An hour later, sated and humming, she rode the elevator back upstairs to get her coat. It wasn't far to the train station; she was going to walk over and see if her painting carrier had turned up.

Eighth floor, third room down the hall to the left. She was startled to see the door ajar, then realized the housekeeper must be inside. The woman had knocked several times during the morning and early afternoon, leaving silently when Hanna called out, "Go away, please. Come back later." She went in, ready to apologize for delaying the cleaning schedule.

The room was in chaos. Clothes tumbled on the floor, the easel box agape, paint tubes everywhere. Someone had used alizarin crimson to scrawl BITCH across the mirror on the closet door. Hanna ran to the bathroom, grabbed a towel, and rubbed the words into an unintelligible smear.

Numbed by a feeling of unreality, she fumbled through her possessions with unmanageable fingers. As far as she could tell nothing was missing.

Her coat had been stuffed under the bed, inside out. She

retrieved it and saw that a long slit had been cut in the lining. She put it on anyway and grabbed the purse she had carried to lunch, then slammed the door and ran along the hall. Too impatient to wait for an elevator, she clattered down the stairs and into the lobby.

At the entrance she stopped long enough to stuff her hair into a knit cap. She had to get outside, breathe some fresh air, and work off a head of steam. She was mad. Damn mad.

It was sleeting. Ice pellets, driven by blustery wind, worried at her clothing like a dog with a bone. Good, weather to match her mood. She shook her head when the doorman motioned for a taxi, and got a look that expressed his opinion of her mental capacity.

The sleet ceased as though someone had turned off a faucet as she neared the train station. The wind hushed, huge, papery snowflakes slipstreamed past her face. A sudden whim made her put out her tongue and catch one. She felt better.

The station was almost deserted, there was no one behind the Lost and Found counter. She walked to her locker and extracted the key from her purse, then fumbled at the lock with cold-stiffened fingers. Finally she made it work and opened the squealing metal door. Her sketch pad was on top, she looked at the drawing of Fur-coat. He scowled back.

Maybe he's here in Basel. Maybe he and the Cro-Magnons found out where I'm staying and trashed my room, just for the hell of it. She thought of the vanished painting carrier. Suspicion flowered. Suppose they. . . .

Stop it! You're not living a Mary Stewart novel. You lost the carrier, left it on the train, probably. Careless.

What about my room, a stubborn voice rebutted. That's real enough.

She closed the locker and began walking. Oh, Christian would love this, all right. After she'd told him with such lofty assurance how efficient she was at managing her own affairs. She could just hear him. "So everyone changes, do they, my love?"

At last she found a door marked with the familiar international symbol of a female stick figure. Inside was a neat, impersonal facility with white walls and old-fashioned porcelain sinks. She walked to a mirror and pulled off her cap.

Thick wet hair tumbled around her face, the gold-red color dulled to wet brown. She found paper towels and blotted moisture off her cheeks and forehead, then caught the hair up and squeezed out as much water as she could.

She leaned close to the mirror to see if her eyes looked as bloodshot as they felt, after the sleepless night. No, they were okay, the whites sharply defined against skin tanned on the Ibizan beach, the smoky irises almost black. Even her eyelashes were wet, they clumped together in dark spikes.

She pulled a fat-toothed yellow comb out of her purse and set to work on the tangle of hair. When most of the snarls were unraveled, she made a single thick braid behind her head and fastened it with an elastic band.

Smearing a little gloss over dry lips, she walked out into the corridor. A cup of coffee would save her life. Hot, black, and fragrant. She moved with the energy of a woman on a mission, unable to resist watching people with an artist's curious eye as she looked for an open refreshment stand.

It wasn't an evening for frivolous travel. Those whom circumstance had forced away from home were so heavily bundled in coats, hats, and scarves they reminded her of primitive wooden figures.

Most of the business stalls were closed and dark, their entrances padlocked behind iron grills. Finally she saw a lighted cubicle at the far end of the passage. She hurried past window displays and bulletin boards pasted with fliers and notices to stand behind a man buying a newspaper from the proprietress. He honored Hanna with a cursory glance, then continued talking to the fat, red-faced woman behind the counter.

He irritated her. Sleek, dry, comfortable, he wore a trim black ski jacket and visored, military-style cap. The conversation extended, the fat woman looked at Hanna and made a comment to the man. He answered and laughed.

That did it. She didn't understand German beyond a few tourist phrases, but any idiot could see they were talking about her. She cleared her throat. "Excuse me, but when you've finished your chat I'd like to buy something."

Maybe he wouldn't understand her words, but her meaning was sure as hell obvious.

The man moved aside, sketched a mocking bow, and allowed her access to the counter. They engaged in a brief stare-down contest, then he broke eye contact and walked away.

"Bitte?" the proprietress prodded.

Hanna asked for coffee.

The sow shook her head. *"Nein, nein."*

Pointing to a candy bar, Hanna said "chocolate" and laid down a Swiss franc. The sullen lump made change, her dewlaps shaking as she counted to herself. Hanna scooped up coins and candy and muttered "bitch," as she left the counter.

She walked toward an outside door, unwrapping the candy. What was she going to do about the hotel room? Properly she should notify the desk and ask them to call the police, she supposed. Her blood pressure escalated. What good would that do? They'd sympathize, ask a few questions, and that would be that. She was a tourist, she hadn't been hurt and nothing was stolen. The police had more important things to worry about.

A waste of time, mine and theirs. I'll clean up the mess and go on about my business.

That decided, she relaxed. It was pleasant in the train station, and a little impersonal company suited her. Why not stay awhile? She might even get a pad and some conté crayons out of her locker and sketch after she finished her candy.

She walked to an area of nearly deserted benches and chose a place. Eating slowly, she savored the perfume of the rich chocolate, felt it slide down her throat with the enjoyment only pure sin can offer.

A young mother, tired and scolding, took refuge on a nearby

bench. She was trying without too much success to restrain an energetic young imp. He was a pretty child, four or five years old; he made Hanna remember the sketch pad. She grinned at him.

An audience was all he needed. He pulled away from his mother and advanced, a few steps at a time, flirting through fingers across his eyes.

Hanna pulled her face into a conspiratorial wink.

He responded with a mischievous laugh and ran to fling himself in her lap, then changed his mind and veered off, holding his arms up for airplane wings. Out of his mouth came the universal engine noises little boys are born knowing how to make.

His mother called "Claude," and he banked in her direction, then tripped over a man with outstretched feet, buried in a newspaper.

Claude howled. His mother jumped up. The man dropped his paper and lifted the downed airplane, who promptly flung off assisting arms and headed for Mamma.

She shook him, scolding and petting at the same time. The boy pointed at Hanna and wailed "chocolate." Mamma sighed and got up, he pulled her toward the newsstand.

Hanna was vaguely aware of the departure of Claude and Mamma, but her attention was on the man who had once again shrouded himself in the London *Times*. Damned if it wasn't the same rude devil who had delayed her at the newsstand. What did he do, loiter around train stations insulting women and tripping children for a hobby?

She finished her candy, leaned back, and closed her eyes. No danger of falling asleep, the seat was about as comfortable as a church pew.

Her thoughts drifted to Ibiza, the beach. She could go back. Christian would tease, Malika would simply shrug and accept the change of plans in her tranquil way.

I'm off to a bad start in Basel. Maybe I will go back to Ibiza.

Like hell I will.

F·O·U·R

A SINGLE drab taxi waited at the stand when Hanna left the station. She raised a hand to flag it, then saw the huddled figures crammed inside. The driver slammed a door and drove away as she watched.

Well, who cared, exercise was good for her. She started off toward the hotel. It ought to be easy enough to hail a cab along the way, meanwhile, walking wasn't unpleasant. The wind had quieted and the snow stopped, leaving a thin, crunchy deposit on the streets.

A simple explanation for her ransacked room occurred to her. She'd just checked in to the hotel the evening before, her room must have been vacated by some rich, flashy type who sent out come-hither signals to a burglar.

Just goes to show, never put off until tomorrow what you can do today. Shiftless thief, he wasn't even efficient at making a dishonest living. She wished she could have seen his face when he broke in a day late and found nothing but painting gear and a few clothes for his trouble. No wonder he scrawled BITCH on the mirror.

As for the mess, it wouldn't be the first time she'd cleaned one up. Her studio at home always looked worse than that the week before a one-man show.

She didn't feel good about staying on in the same place, though; the incident had left a bad taste in her mouth. She remembered a scrap of conversation during her visit with Christian and Malika. At a late island dinner she'd met a French couple, the Blanchevilles, who owned the Ibizan newspaper. Talk got around to Switzerland, Cecile Blancheville raved about a wonderful place in Basel where she and Claude stayed during a press convention.

The Hotel Ange Noir—the Black Angel. Hanna thought it sounded like a natural habitat for Marlene Dietrich. Cecile described it with vivid Gallic gestures; sixteenth century, gables, a cobblestone courtyard. Close to the Rhine; and best of all, according to the thrifty Frenchwoman, not so expensive you couldn't enjoy.

It was still early evening. Hanna decided to phone the Ange Noir, if they had a vacant room she'd throw her things together and move tonight.

After several blocks her long strides slowed to a stop. Nothing looked familiar. Had she gotten disoriented in the twisting streets and made a wrong turn? This area was almost deserted; no pedestrians, no moving traffic, only a few parked cars scattered in a desultory manner. Better retrace her route back to the train station.

Before she could, headlights blinded her. A black Mercedes out of nowhere advanced on her in eerie silence, its distinctive hood ornament gleaming.

She moved closer to a building. The street was narrow, closed in by dingy, hovering buildings. The Mercedes picked up speed and hurtled at her. She stood transfixed, feeling like a rabbit pinned in the beam of a hunter's spotlight.

Tires squealed. The car rocked to a stop, its right rear door burst open, and a man spilled out. That was enough for Hanna, she ran. Rough hands caught her shoulders, pulling her off her feet and backward against a body hard as a granite statue. She felt herself being lifted.

"No! Let me go!"

She meant to yell, but was shocked to hear a pitiful bleat instead. She struggled; bit, kicked, anything to keep from being stuffed into the maw of that car.

One mammoth arm slid around her waist, another circled her throat in a stranglehold. She jabbed with a vicious right elbow and felt it dig into the soft spot just below his breast bone. He spewed threats as he dragged her toward the car.

She clawed at the vise around her throat. He tried to pin her arms, but she managed to keep one free and groped behind her head for his eyes. When that failed she drew up her knees, arched her back, and kicked out. Maybe she could throw him off balance.

The grip on her neck tightened. She bit his arm, then lashed out with her elbow again; this time the blow slid harmlessly off an iron rib cage. She was possessed by recklessness born of desperation, better be killed now than find out what was waiting for her inside that silent hearse.

A shout rose behind them. The mouth against her ear cursed, Hanna forced out a muffled shriek. A voice inside the Mercedes barked commands as running footsteps approached. She felt the man who held her convulse and expel breath with the hissing sound of an angry cobra.

Another set of arms pulled at her. For agonizing seconds she felt like a rag doll being ripped apart by wicked children, then she was free and dropped to the ground, sucking in great ragged gulps of air. The Mercedes' engine roared and echoed in the narrow street, to the music of squealing tires.

"You're safe. Easy now, they've gone."

The voice spoke English, firm hands helped her stand. She tried to thank whoever it was, but convulsive sobs welled from the pit of her stomach. Her legs shook.

He patted her back with awkward concern.

"You're a big girl. Tall, I mean. Tall girl. I can hold you up, I think. Or we'll go down together." Sudden suspicion made him draw away. "You aren't going to be sick, are you?"

Hanna shook her head and hoped it was the truth.

"Breathe slow and easy, everything's going to be all right. Okay, that's right, that's it." The words were automatic, soothing. "Can you walk if I help?"

"Give me a minute," she gasped, and leaned against the rough stone wall of an adjacent building.

They were midblock, it was very dark. Mist haloed a street lamp on the corner, silhouetting a compact, muscular man. He pulled out a pack of cigarettes and cupped his hands, a lighter flared. Hanna saw his face.

"You were at the train station."

"I was?" The words were half question, half agreement.

"At the newsstand, chatting up that fat sow. Then you were hiding behind the *Times* when you tripped that child."

"You mean Claude, the airplane boy?"

"Are you following me?"

"Hey, I didn't attack you, remember? I'm the good guy."

"True," Hanna admitted reluctantly. She was in no mood to accept things at face value. Where the hell had he come from, out of nowhere?

Her suspicions were interrupted by a sudden blast of voices and laughter. Up the street three men spilled onto the pavement from a tavern. One mimicked a popular singer in an exaggerated falsetto, his friends were convulsed.

As they neared, the singer broke off. He stared at Hanna and the man with the open curiosity of a drunk and asked a question, his voice slurring the German syllables.

Hanna's companion answered in the same language. The singer laughed and repeated the reply to his friends. They slapped each other with knowing winks and snickered, then walked on. A different troubadour took up the song.

"What did you say to him?"

"He asked if we were having a lovers' quarrel. I told him you were about to get into a car with another man when I caught you. I said I swatted your ass a couple of times to teach you a lesson."

"How clever. Glad everyone had a good laugh."

That was bitchy, he'll wish he'd let the Mercedes gang have me.

"I haven't thanked you," she said, with the sincerity of a chicken eyeballing a frying pan. "You might have been hurt yourself."

He shrugged. "What else could I do, you were assaulted right under my nose. You run with a tough crowd."

"I run with . . . I don't know who that was! Some of the guys, bored on a slow Saturday night. Thought they'd liven up the evening by kidnapping a woman. Who the hell knows?"

"Looks like they could have found a better candidate. The typical female victim, you're not."

Hanna stopped and gave him a withering look.

"Okay, okay, don't get your feathers ruffled. Mere statement of fact, not a slur. Feel any better?" He changed the subject. "The merrymakers came out of a bar, let's go slosh something down. Cauterize your throat and warm your gut. We can continue this verbal joust just as well sitting, can't we?"

As they walked Hanna felt him staring.

God, I must be beautiful.

She was battered, bruised, and truculent. Her throat hurt. She felt about as sociable as a Tasmanian Devil. Okay, she'd have one brandy to be polite and then it was so long, Lone Ranger.

She remembered about moving to the Ange Noir.

To hell with it. Sufficient unto the day is the action thereof, or something like that.

A single naked bulb illuminated the ancient stone and wood of the tavern entrance. Just below was a small, shield-shaped sign which depicted a white leopard leering rakishly and raising a triumphant beer stein.

They walked in. Blessed warmth from the softly lit room enveloped them, carrying the yeasty aroma of lager ale. A worn, plank floor supported tile-topped tables and wooden chairs. Candles flickered here and there, revealing heads bent together in conversation or affection.

They sat at a table by the bar. A yellow-haired waitress, scantily costumed in a short Tyrolean skirt and peasant blouse, stopped bantering with the bartender and sauntered over to Hanna's companion.

"Two Courvoisiers, please."

The waitress nodded, scowled at Hanna, and undulated away, her lovely body swaying as if to an imagined rendition of "Bolero."

Her mating dance seemed lost on the man from the train station, who was fumbling for cigarettes. He found them and offered the pack to Hanna, she brushed it away with an impatient hand.

"Not a smoker? Mind if I do?"

She shook her head.

"I'm trying to cut down." He lit up and touched his match to the candle on their table. The wick flared and relaxed to a steady pinpoint of light.

The waitress came back with brandies in record time. She ignored Hanna and leaned over the man, murmuring in a husky voice.

She did have a magnificent body, Hanna grudgingly admitted. Her legs were long and shapely under the tiny skirt, her breasts revealed in perilous splendor by the low-cut blouse. They throbbed in twin perfection, two inches from the man's face.

He had the grace to look self-conscious as he put a handful of coins on the table. The waitress scooped them up and left.

"I thought Lorelei there was going to drop the money down her front and offer you a chance to retrieve it with your teeth. Friend of yours?" Hanna asked.

He grinned. "An acquaintance. Her name's Marga. Which reminds me, I don't know yours."

"Hanna Anders."

"I'm Clete Cross. American, a banker. Besides ogling waitresses and rescuing the odd female in distress, I'm in Basel for a meeting with Swiss associates. You here on business or pleasure?"

"Both. I'm an artist. I came to paint, and to . . . look around."

"You came to Basel to paint?"

"Why do you say it like that?"

"I'd have thought an artist would head straight for the mountain villages. More picturesque than a large city, aren't they? Besides, most Americans never heard of Basel. You must have other reasons for being here, like friends or relatives."

"I—" She almost blurted out the whole business about Dedushka and the inheritance. Not smart, she didn't know this man. To distract him she touched her throat and made a face.

He took the bait. "Hurt bad?"

She shook her head and affected a hoarse tone. "No, but it's getting harder to talk."

"Let me see." He pulled his chair around, put a hand on her shoulder and tilted her chin.

His scrutiny made Hanna feel squirmy, but it didn't keep her from examining the face so close to her nearsighted eyes. His were cat's eyes, hazel, with flecks of metallic green clustered around pupils she half expected to be elliptical. They were wide-set, above a strong nose that was slightly crooked, as if it had been broken. His mouth had a beautiful curve, rescued from being feminine by a strong, no-nonsense chin.

She wanted to see his hair, but the damn cap hid it. He seemed to sense her frustration and took it off, releasing unruly brown curls.

"It's hard to tell much about your neck in this light. You'll have some severe bruising. You ought to see a doctor."

She ignored the suggestion. "You don't look like a banker."

"What? Oh. Sorry to disappoint you. What do bankers look like?"

She waved a dismissive hand. "I don't mean a stereotype. It's just . . . oh, I don't know."

He leaned closer. "Let's talk about you. You haven't said whether you have friends or family here."

What makes you so curious? Hanna wondered. She reached for her glass. It was empty.

"Want another?"

"Better not, I haven't eaten in hours. What I really need is a taxi. I'm beat, I want to fall in bed and sleep the clock around."

He put a hand on her arm. "Hanna, let me help. You're in some kind of trouble. . . ."

She began a denial, he raised a flat palm. "Yes you are, realize it or not.

"Listen, I walked to the train station earlier to pick up a paper, that's why you saw me there. I was on my way back to the Leopard when I saw you being dragged off by what you say was the local sex maniac.

"Now. I have a rental car parked nearby and I'm offering to transport you safely to your destination. There's nothing more important on my agenda tonight than flirting with Marga. Isn't that a handsome offer?"

Hanna thought about it. It was.

"I accept. Sorry if I've been acting like a bitch. I'm not usually surly, but this has been a bad day all around.

"I still don't buy your assumption I'm in trouble, though. Why would anyone want to kidnap me?"

He shrugged. "How should I know?"

She let it drop. "I'm staying at the Olympia."

As they left the table she couldn't resist one last jab. "Wasn't it a coincidence you came along at exactly the right time, back there?"

He shrugged. "Yes, wasn't it? Luck, I guess. Or your Guardian Angel."

F·I·V·E

FOUR hours later Clete returned to a crowded Leopard Tavern. A drift of smoke hung in the air, someone played the piano with the sure touch of a professional. A contralto voice paid tribute to a mellow old blues tune.

He felt good. His senses were fine-tuned, adrenaline pumped through his body with the punch of a shot of speed. Like always, at the beginning of a job.

Marga appeared at his side. "Your friend is here. He asked for a quiet table, I put him in the corner. You see?"

She pointed and touched his arm. *"Liebchen?"*

He patted her firm, curved bottom. "What?"

"Later, you will be rid of him? We can be together, like last night?"

"Hard to tell, sweetheart. Frank and I have some business to take care of."

Marga pouted. "That great, skinny bitch with the red hair, she was not business." Her breast caressed his arm. "I will make you forget her. Come to me. I will wait. If it is late, I do not mind."

"We'll see, *Liebchen*, we'll see."

Clete spotted Frank Rivera's narrow, sad face across the room. As he weaved through the crowd he thought for the millionth time how Frank looked like a painting of a Spanish saint by Velázquez; one of those weird guys who flagellated themselves and wore hair shirts. He'd never mentioned the resemblance to Frank.

"Been here long?" He settled into the second chair.

Frank shrugged. "Long enough. Did you put the woman to bed?"

"In a manner of speaking. There are some interesting developments." He looked at Marga, who had followed him to the table.

"Bring me a lager, gorgeous."

She left, her parts jiggling in tantalizing harmony.

Frank whistled under his breath. "Thirty seconds more and she'd have jumped your bones in front of God and everybody. What is it you do to women, Clete?"

Clete shrugged and tried to look modest. "Poor girl's just starved for a little attention. No time for that tonight, though."

He told Frank about the attack on Hanna.

Frank ruffled his tonsured fringe and sighed. "Hippolyte the Hulk. So the big boss sicked him on her. Was Octavian in the car himself, do you think? If they recognized you, it'll hit the fan. Maybe you shoulda let 'em have her. Keep 'em occupied awhile, so they won't notice us."

Marga came, carrying a Pilsner glass filled with foaming amber liquid. She set it in front of Clete, her motor running. He waved a firm good-bye and answered Frank.

"No, I want her loose. I think she can answer some questions."

"Didn't you get anything out of her?"

"Not damn-all so far. Her story is, she's an innocent American artist, in Basel to paint pictures."

"Bullshit."

"Yeah. Question's not *if* she's involved, but how. First we see her in Geneva, running for the train with Octavian and his bully boys in hot pursuit. Then we get to Basel, dodging the sleazoids, and you spot one of them making off with part of her luggage."

"It was a homemade deal," Frank put in. "Some kind of wooden crate with a handle and screening on two sides. Why in hell would they want that?"

"I don't know, but whatever they were after, they don't have it yet. Octavian was pretty desperate to try a no-class street snatch like that. Not his style.

"Back to the girl. She let me escort her to her hotel, then decided she was going to move. Right then. She made a call from a lobby phone, for a reservation."

"In front of you?"

"Oh, she tried to get rid of me, but I wouldn't budge. I said I had a stake in her welfare, since I'd rescued her once already. She stopped short of telling me to get lost, she's too well-mannered for that."

"More fool, she," Frank muttered.

"Her first mistake was letting it slip she was going to change hotels. I insisted on taking her. She gave in, then tried to get me to wait in the lobby while she packed. I didn't go for it. I said I better escort her upstairs, make sure no one was hiding in her room.

"It was a mess, Frank. Someone did a real number on it. She wasn't surprised, either, it was obvious she'd already seen it."

"No wonder she wanted to leave. Where'd you take her?"

"A place called the Ange Noir. Piece of luck; it's in the old section, not far from where we're staying."

"Think you were followed?"

"I'm sure we weren't. Careless of Octavian."

Frank rubbed his eyes. "God, I'm tired." He downed the last of his beer and held up the glass to catch Marga's attention.

"I'm worried, Clete. You know I don't like tangling with Octavian, he's got more damn tentacles than an octopus. And I think it's time you gave me the full rundown on this business. Remember, all I know so far is an old bird named Madeleine

Anderson died in Philadelphia, and we're after something she stashed here before World War II. You never mentioned Octavian being mixed up in the deal."

"I'm not keeping you in the dark. I wish to hell I knew what brought him here."

"It can't be coincidence."

"Sure it can. His old mother lives in Basel, he's paying a duty call."

"Oh, right."

"Forget Octavian a few minutes. I'll tell you the whole story about Madeleine Anderson.

"She was a Russian blue blood. Daughter of a cousin of the last Tsar. You know, Nicholas.

"Anderson's parents managed to have her smuggled out of Russia at the beginning of the Revolution. A family friend, woman by the name of Ilse Bonnard who came from Basel, brought her back here.

"There was one other child, a boy, who had been shipped off to America earlier. Just before World War II he managed to trace Anderson. He came, they must have had a grand reunion, and he took her back to the States."

"Could we get past the history and genealogy?"

"Be patient. Ever hear of Carl Fabergé?"

"Guy who made Easter eggs out of gold and jewels?"

"That's him. He's famous for the eggs, but he did a lot of other stuff, too. In 1915 he was commissioned by the Tsar for a special job."

Clete bit off a chunk of buttery pretzel and continued.

"Those Orthodox Russians were very religious people. The Tsar was no exception. There he was, nailed to the cross by a war with Kaiser Wilhelm, and the Bolsheviks were beginning to rip hell out of his home front. His heir to the throne was a sickly hemophiliac, a little kid. He had four daughters, but no other boys. Got the picture?"

Frank grunted.

"So. Someone had given him three little religious paintings, dating from the fourteenth century. The Tsar asked Fabergé to design and make a triptych to hold them. Gave him carte blanche to do up the fanciest setting he could imagine. When it was finished Tsar Nicholas was going to give it to the Church, to buy prayers for victory in the German war, and his son's recovery."

"Swell. What's that got to do with the old lady in Philly?"

"I told you, her father was the Tsar's cousin. I'll get to that part.

"By the time Fabergé finished the triptych, Nicholas was in deep trouble. Trying to lead his troops on the German front, and dashing home as often as possible to put out Bolshevik brush fires.

"Then there was his wife Alexandra, and a mad monk named Rasputin . . . but that's another story," he added hastily as Frank's eyes rolled heavenward.

"With the monarchy floundering, blue-blooded rats were abandoning the sinking ship of state at a fast clip. Paris or New York were healthier. But what was Tsar Nicky going to do, hop a train with his family and leave, carrying the state treasury?"

"The answer is no, I take it," Frank said wearily. "This whole damn thing fascinates you, doesn't it?"

"Yeah, I guess it does. Anyway, for some reason Cousin Peter, Madeleine Anderson's father, was given the Fabergé triptych. He and his wife disappeared during the Revolution, but the triptych had been sent to Switzerland with Madeleine."

"Has anyone seen it since? Do we have any idea what it looks like? And why in hell would she leave it here; why didn't she and her brother take it to the States? It all sounds like some half-baked fairy tale to me."

"Swear to God, Frank, it's not. I can't answer your last question; who knows why they left it here? I have reliable information they did, though.

"And we do know what it looks like. Several weeks ago an art book, one of those glossy deals that costs a hundred bucks a copy, came out. It was made up of a bio on Fabergé, and photos of all his documented pieces.

"There were two snaps of the triptych, old, taken by a goldsmith in the studio workroom. Black and white, front and back.

"Even in a fuzzy print without color, the thing is enough to make any collector drool. The author made a big mystery about how it had dropped out of sight several decades ago."

"Yeah?"

Clete rubbed the stubble on his jaw. "Anderson was alive when the guy wrote the book, but he didn't mention her. He must not have known anything about her part in the deal, or else he was sworn to secrecy."

He slapped the table.

"Sonofabitch! I just remembered something, Frank. I read somewhere that the author was killed in a one-car accident 'under mysterious circumstances,' right after his book was published."

Frank looked bleak. "Octavian."

"We're not backing down, Frank. We can fade the heat. We'll get the triptych and nail Octavian's ass to the wall too, if we're lucky."

"Big talk," Frank jeered.

"I mean it. You may think I'm loony tunes, but remember I have a score to settle with that crazy bastard. He'll slip up one of these days, and I'm gonna be there to grind his face into the dirt when it happens."

"Aren't you forgetting a few details? Like he has unlimited money and a regiment of international scumbags?"

Clete smiled engagingly. "We're smarter."

"Sure, that's why he has millions and we live by the seat of our pants. I do, anyway, not having inherited a bundle, like some people."

Clete knew it was time to talk about something else. It was never a good idea to let Frank brood about Octavian for long.

"Tell me about your day. Did you get anywhere with the name I gave you? Ilse Bonnard?"

"Twelve Bonnards in the phone directory. No Ilse, but if she was the friend who brought Madeleine Anderson out of Russia she'd be dead by now." Frank pulled a notebook out of his pocket and put on a small pair of reading glasses.

"I went to all twelve addresses, Clete. Three Bonnards out of town. At one of those places I talked to the housekeeper, at two I got some information from neighbors.

"At a couple more spots people refused to talk to me. Of the other seven, no one admitted having heard of Ilse Bonnard or Madeleine Anderson."

"What about the street name I gave you, Stillestrasse?"

"None of them lived there, or even close. I asked everyone I talked to if their family had ever lived on Stillestrasse, all I got were negatives."

"Someone could be lying."

"Sure, but why? I cooked up a story about a small inheritance from a distant relative of Ilse Bonnard's in the United States. Most of them seemed anxious to help. The man and woman who refused to talk at all lived in shacks, I can't believe the Tsar's cousin would have sent his daughter to a slum."

"And the ones who were out of town?"

"Two had posh addresses. The housekeeper I talked with was cooperative, but she'd never heard of Ilse Bonnard, and she's been with the family for eighteen years.

"The other place was a flat in an old mansion, very chic. The neighbors said a young couple lives there. They had the impression the man didn't come from Basel."

Clete shook his head. "No help at all." He rubbed his forehead, thinking.

"Frank, I'll watch Hanna Anders during the day tomorrow. I want you to go to Stillestrasse and become intimately acquainted with every inch of it. Talk to people, try to find out if there were ever any Bonnards there."

Frank sighed. "I hope it's a short street, I left my corn plasters at home.

"Back to Hanna baby. Where do you think she fits in?"

Clete shrugged. "I can make all sorts of guesses. She might be an ex-employee of Octavian's who's branched out on her own. Or maybe she was the girlfriend of the guy who wrote the book on Fabergé."

"I don't think she worked for Octavian," Frank said. "If she did they wouldn't bother kidnapping her, she'd be found in a ditch with her throat cut. Could she be some relative of Anderson's?"

"That's certainly a possibility. Anderson never married, but we don't know much about the brother, except he's dead. I'll call the States, have someone check on it.

"Incidentally, did I tell you I'm taking Hanna to dinner tomorrow night? No graceful way she could refuse, me saving her life, and all."

"You'll have her cooing like a turtle dove."

"Not much chance of that, I'll have to watch my step. She didn't take me at face value, for sure. She accused me of following her from the train station."

"Suspicious broad. What kind of a scam did you lay on her?"

"Told her I'm a banker, here on business. If I can put her at ease she might let something slip."

"She'd better for her own sake, with Octavian snarling at her heels. She could get hurt."

Frank counted out a tip for Marga.

Clete added some money to Frank's pile, stood and stretched. "You're right. She could sure as hell get hurt."

S·I·X

HER parents were at it again. Fighting in the bedroom, voices clearly audible through the thin partition that separated their room from Hanna's. Her father's placating rumble was drowned in the deluge of words spewed out by her mother, words that stung like wasps in a honey jar.

That voice. Hanna thought how astonished Caroline Anders' friends would be, if they could hear the dulcet, southern-belle tones raised to a shrewish shriek. She felt a desperate urge to escape. Leave the house for a long hike, or take her accustomed refuge in Dedushka's room at the end of the hall.

She couldn't, not this time. It was Dedushka they were fighting about, she had to stay and listen.

"I mean it. I won't have him here another week. Not another day. There are perfectly good places right here in Denver, where he can be with other old men in the same shape. And where he'll be watched, so he can't burn the damn place down, or wander off and get lost.

"Don't oppose me on this, Nick, or you'll be sorry. I'm sick of him. You're gone all day, you don't know . . . no one should be forced to put up with what I do."

Nick Anders' reply was short, indistinguishable.

There was a connecting door between the two bedrooms; Hanna gripped the knob. Her hands were clammy, an iron band constricted her lungs. She looked down, the worn blue of her sweatshirt convulsed each time her heart beat.

It was forbidden to interrupt a "discussion" between her parents.

She had to risk it. Her mother wanted to send Dedushka to an old folk's home to die, with no one for company but strangers.

Still she lingered, gathering courage and rehearsing her plea.

Mustn't say "Dedushka" in front of her mother. "There'll be no Russian spoken in this family, young lady. He's your grandpa and that's what you'll call him as long as you're under my roof."

She pushed through the door and walked straight to her father, careful not to look in her mother's direction.

"Daddy, don't send Grandpa away, it'll kill him. He's careful with his pipe, he'll stop smoking it if you ask him. And he's never wandered off, he just likes to be by himself sometimes. There's nothing wrong with that."

Nick Anders patted his daughter's shoulder. At fourteen she was as tall as he.

"There are lots of things you're too young to understand, baby. I know you love him—"

Her mother interrupted, furious.

"You stay out of this, young lady. It's none of your business. And really, Hanna, a girl tall as a man shouldn't cry, it makes you look half-witted. Leave tears to the cute little things. Now straighten up your face and get out of this room."

I hate you. Words that trembled in the air between mother and daughter; terrible, unspoken.

Hanna struggled through layers of sleep toward the blessed relief of consciousness. Dreams about her mother had become less frequent over the years, but they still evoked the same mixture of misery, pain, and bitterness.

Caroline Anders. Petite and camellia pretty, her whole life had been an anticlimax since the day she was Homecoming Queen at the University of Alabama. She had bitterly resented her only child. Hanna remembered herself, a tall, quiet girl who loved to spend long hours in her grandfather's room and hear his stories, or to roam the mountains with her lunch, her paint box, and a book in her pocket.

Caroline had hated her, all right. Goaded her under the guise of motherly concern.

"Why don't you make some friends? Join the pep club, try out for cheerleader?"

Hanna had a mental picture of herself; tall, bony frame herky-jerky with a cheerleader's gyrations.

"Where can that size have come from? And that red hair? It has to be some kind of glandular problem, I don't care what the doctor says. Well, you must make the best of it. Stand up straight.

"When I was your age, oh, the boys that hung around our house. Couldn't stir 'em with a stick, my daddy said.

"I don't expect you to be able . . . but you could at least try. Wear something besides those jeans and boots. Put a ribbon in your hair, flirt a little. Aren't there any tall boys in school?"

Hanna had almost allowed herself to drift back into the nightmare again, hearing the old, acid words that were etched into her brain. She sat up, reached for her robe.

Funny she never dreamed about the horrible thing. Didn't even think about it much anymore.

Six years ago, the summer between college graduation and her planned departure for New York City and art school. Nick and Caroline Anders lying on the bedroom floor. Caroline's breast a bloody mess. Nick's face shot off, the gun near his lifeless fingers. Murder and suicide.

She stumbled to the bathroom, stepped into clouds of steam in a hot shower and washed away the past.

When her body was buffed rosy with soft terry towels, Hanna inspected her throat in the mirror above the lavatory. Impressive bruising, darker on the right side. It hurt to swallow. Her muscles protested every moment, sending angry pain signals to her brain. In all, though, she was in good shape for someone who'd been mugged by the Incredible Hulk's doppelganger.

She put in her contact lenses. Her face was puffy; she traced a broken blood vessel below her right eye with a curious finger.

Her temper built up a head of steam as she dressed. Nobody, no army for that matter, was going to scare her out of Basel. She came here because of a promise to Dedushka. A little late, maybe, but now she was here she would stay until she got some answers.

Flopping into her favorite cross-legged position on the bed, she took a small velvet box out of her purse, extracted a ring, and held it to the light.

The central stone was a large, emerald-cut sapphire, surrounded by clusters of smaller sapphires and diamonds in a setting of yellow gold. It was enameled and engraved with Russian script.

The large stone was very rare in color and size. Not the deep royal blue of most sapphires; it was a variety that came from Ceylon, and was prized for its brilliant sky hue. She had been a college freshman home on spring break when Dedushka gave her the ring.

"This will identify you to the family in Switzerland who holds your inheritance. As I have told you, my sister never married. Since she has no heirs, you, my one grandchild, are the only descendant of a very noble family.

"You are grown now, you must go to Basel as soon as possible. It should be safe after all these years. But be careful, child, very careful. Tell no one what you find in the box, bring it back to America and get a lawyer, a good one. He can tell you how to proceed."

Dedushka had died six weeks later. She got the news by telegram, read it on the way to an American Lit. seminar.

Slipping the ring on her finger, she walked to a window and looked out. Brilliant sun slanted across the courtyard, only the deepest shadows clung to melting traces of dirty snow.

Memories again. The years that had flown by. College, her parents' terrible deaths, art school. Then hard work to establish herself as a professional artist. The urgency of Dedushka's quest had faded, his stories took on the rich, warm hues of her favorite childhood adventures. *Treasure Island* or *The Prince and the Pauper*.

She left the window and picked up the telephone to make one more try at speaking with her grandfather's sister in Philadelphia, Madeleine Anderson. Strange, mysterious woman, living so far away from Denver. Never communicating with her relatives.

Hanna remembered Dedushka's funeral, Nick Anders cursing the aunt who hadn't bothered to send condolences at the death of her only brother. Hanna had asked if he'd ever met Aunt Madeleine. He nodded.

"I don't remember much about her. She and Dad had a terrible fight when I was six or seven. They never spoke again, as far as I know. But he's dead, for God's sake, and she's old. We're all the family she has."

Before Hanna departed for Europe she had written to the woman. No response. On the eve of her departure she telephoned. A female voice answered, identified itself as Miss Anderson's friend, and said Miss Anderson was ill and would not talk to anyone.

Now Hanna placed the call again, determined not to be put off. The connection went through.

"Hello?" The same voice as before.

"My name is Hanna Anders, I'm calling from Switzerland,

I'm Miss Anderson's grand-niece. I must talk with her, it's urgent."

Silence; drawn out so long Hanna began to suspect the connection had been broken. Then, "I'm sorry, Miss Anders, Madeleine is dead. She died last week."

Hanna closed her eyes and sighed. "I'm sorry to hear that. Could you tell me what happened to her belongings?"

"I was her only friend, I've taken care of her for years. She never mentioned any family.

"If you're thinking about money, you can forget it. Everything she had went to the Church, except personal possessions. She left them to me. It's precious little, I can tell you." The woman's voice was defensive.

"I'm not interested in money, or anything like that," Hanna assured her. "Family papers, photographs, something that would shed light on her life before she came to the United States . . . did you find that sort of thing?"

Before the woman could answer Hanna added, "You say you looked after her for years? Was she an invalid?"

"Not exactly. She was kinda squirrely, you know, had been for ages. Oh, strong enough physically. Part of the time she made sense when she talked, but mostly she just rattled on." The voice sounded less hostile.

"She was lucky to have someone like you to care for her."

"That's true, she was. We got acquainted after my husband died and I moved into the flat downstairs. She was older'n me; and sharp enough, then. She had time on her hands. She started inviting me up for afternoon coffee and cake."

"About family papers, did she leave any?"

"Nothing. Not a scrap of paper or a photograph. I wondered myself, it did seem peculiar. But then her being an immigrant. . . ."

Dead end. Hanna tried to think of something that might bring forth information.

"Mrs. . . . what is your name?"

"O'Connor."

"Mrs. O'Connor, did she ever mention Switzerland to you?"

The woman answered slowly. "Yes, that does sound familiar. She lived there once, didn't she?"

"That's right. Did she ever mention the name Bonnard?"

"Bonnard. I . . . I can't remember. Look, Miss Anders, whatever it is you're getting at, I can't help you. There's a roast in the oven in my apartment downstairs. I have to go."

"Wait . . ." No use, the connection was severed.

Hanna held the buzzing receiver until the operator came on to ask if she wanted to make another call.

What had she learned, apart from the fact her great-aunt had been dead for a week?

Nothing; but a week ago was when she began to feel compulsive about coming to Basel right away. Spooky.

She lay on the bed, laced her fingers behind her head, and began thinking aloud.

"Ilse Bonnard must be dead. What did Dedushka say that will help me find her relatives, if she has any left?

"A school, her family ran an exclusive school for girls. Tante Sophia, that was in the name. Tante Sophia's on . . . Stillestrasse. Silent street."

She picked up the phone and asked for help from the switchboard operator. The school was listed, the operator dialed.

"Oui?" A woman's voice.

"Do you speak English, please? My French is not good."

The cultured voice came back, slightly chilly. "Yes. Who is this? What is it you want?"

As concisely as possible Hanna identified herself and explained about Dedushka and his sister, Madeleine Anderson, leaving out any mention of a family inheritance. She ended by saying, "So you see, I would like to find a relative of Ilse Bonnard's."

"I am Madame Mercier. Ilse Bonnard was my aunt."

"Oh, wonderful! And have you heard of Madeleine Anderson?"

"She lived with us when I was a little girl. I remember her." The admission sounded reluctant.

"Please, may I come see you? Just for a few minutes? I need some information about Madeleine, it's very important."

"I suppose that is possible. But not today, that would not be convenient. Come tomorrow, Monday. Nine o'clock in the morning."

"Thank you very much, I'll be there."

Entering the carpeted brass and crystal cage that served as an elevator, Hanna remembered promising Christian she'd telephone from Basel to let him know she's arrived safely.

I want to thank Malika, too. I'll call for sure, this evening.

The lobby was splendid. Except for unobtrusive business amenities clustered against one wall, it could have been the elegant, comfortable sitting room of a private home. The walls were dark wood, panelled and heavily carved; suspended from the gilt ceiling hung chandeliers of bronze with pearlized handblown glass shades.

The floor was scattered with worn Oriental rugs in blended shades of red and blue. On one side of the room was a giant fireplace around which were several plump easy chairs. A fire burned, a reading table held an assortment of newspapers and magazines.

Hanna walked to the concierge's desk. The man who looked up from an appointment book beamed when he saw her, displaying a prominent gold tooth. He had large, protuberant brown eyes under bushy brows.

"Mademoiselle Anders, good morning. Did you sleep well?"

"You know my name?" Hanna was surprised.

The grin widened. "A beautiful American young lady, tall, with fiery hair? You do not go unnoticed, Mademoiselle. I saw you check in last night. I am Pauli, what may I do for you?"

"I need a rental car, Pauli. Today, if possible. I'm not sure how long I'll want it. Several days. Will that be possible?"

"Of course, Mademoiselle."

He looked toward the door to the dining room. "Are you going to have breakfast with us?"

Hanna grinned. "Yes, I'm starved."

"Then the car will be ready by the time you are finished."

"Thank you, Pauli." Hanna offered a tip, he accepted with a nod of thanks.

There was a bronze plaque on the wall beside the doorway to the dining room, printed in French, German, and English.

> The Hotel Ange Noir was constructed in 1548 as a private residence. In 1730 it was purchased by Franz Lechard; who, after extensive renovation, began operating it as a hostelry. The Hotel is still owned and managed by descendants of Monsieur Lechard.

The middle-age hostess who bustled over to greet her was short and plump. Her eyes gleamed with friendly curiosity, there was a youthful spring to her step.

"Mademoiselle Anders, good morning." She looked around the room. "I will seat you just there, by the doors to the courtyard. It is a beautiful day, you will enjoy the sunshine."

Hanna followed, once again surprised to be called by name.

It was a pleasant table. Sunshine latticed the white linen cloth, there was a cut-glass vase of orange and yellow freesias in the center. She was given a hand-lettered menu, which she looked over while a waitress poured coffee from a silver pot.

Her breakfast arrived. Hanna ate slowly and finished with regret, at loose ends about what to do for the rest of the day. Anything would just be marking time, until tomorrow morning when she could visit Madame Mercier at Tante Sophia's.

Before she left Denver Hanna had researched the Basel area and written for permission to paint in several historical places. Maybe she should ask for a map and guidebook and drive around the old city. Or it might be a good idea to locate Stillestrasse and the school. Or maybe . . . she wondered what Clete Cross was doing.

Put it out of your mind. You're having dinner with him, that's enough. Besides, it's too soon to let him off the hook about his "in the nick of time" rescue. Suppose . . .

Suppose what? Suppose he staged a kidnapping in order to play hero? Why?

Not because he was stricken by my fatal beauty, that's for sure.

"Mademoiselle Anders, you look puzzled. Is there something I can do for you?" The hostess stood at her side.

"No . . . Yes. Could you possibly sit down and have a cup of coffee with me?"

The woman checked her domain, then nodded at a waitress to take her station at the door. "Yes, I believe I can. It is nice of you to invite me."

She sat opposite Hanna and said, "I am Madame Lechard."

"Madame Lechard . . . do you own the hotel? I saw that name on the plaque outside the door. . . ."

The woman nodded with pride, wisps of black hair bounced around her face. "My husband and I. We are all family here. Sylvie, who was on the desk when you arrived, is my niece. Pauli, the concierge, is my sister's husband. It goes on." She made an expansive gesture that seemed to encompass the hotel.

"How wonderful. It's such a lovely place."

They began a polite conversation about weather and travel, subjects to be expected between strangers of different nationalities. Then, during a lull, Hanna heard herself asking, "Do you by any chance know a Madame Mercier?"

Madame Lechard looked startled.

"I'm sorry, that's an impertinent question. It's none of my business; besides, Basel's a large city, you can't know everyone."

"But I do know her, a little. I was surprised for you to mention the name."

"I'm going to meet her tomorrow, and I'm nervous. I need to

talk with her about . . . about a mutual acquaintance. So I phoned for an appointment. Was that rude?"

"Well, if you were not introduced . . . but I am sure she will be charmed by you, once you meet."

"Tell me something about her, please?"

"We are not close friends, but I see her socially, several times a year. Her home was a girls' school, until . . . oh, ten years ago. It had been in the family for many generations, she became Headmistress after her brother died.

"But then, it must have been in the early seventies, she married Monsieur Mercier. He was quite rich, and a hero. He had been a Resistance fighter in France, during World War II. He was older than Helene, of course.

"After they married he became unhappy about the school. He said he wanted her free to travel, but people thought he was jealous of the time she spent with the girls.

"However it was, she closed the school. Monsieur Mercier died . . . six years ago, I believe. He left everything to Helene. She is very wealthy, but it has not made her put on the high hat."

"It sounds like she's led an interesting life."

"Ah, yes. When you meet, tell her you are staying here, and that Madame Lechard conveys her regards. It may be that will help."

"Thank you, I will."

"And how do you occupy yourself this afternoon? Sightseeing, perhaps?"

"I was thinking about it. Pauli's getting me a rental car, but I need a map and guidebook."

"That is no problem, Pauli has those, too. Before you leave, would you like a tour of the hotel? My husband is in Paris on business but I have some free time."

"I'd love it," Hanna said.

S·E·V·E·N

A BACCARAT wine glass shattered against the stone hearth with a satisfying, melodic crash. Octavian picked up another and hurled it.

"Redheaded bitch. Whore. Who the hell is she?" His voice rose with each word.

No one answered. He was alone.

Grabbing the decanter by its neck, he strode to a lead-sheathed casement window and looked out over the tiled roofs of Basel's inner city. Standing with bandied legs apart, he permitted himself to be consumed by spiraling black rage, reducing his intellect to a churning cauldron of seek, kill, devour.

He had felt safe in Switzerland. Maybe let his guard down a little. Enough to allow that bitch to sit under his nose in the Geneva train station and draw a startling likeness of him.

He flung the decanter aside. The stopper fell away, golden wine from his Spanish vineyards gurgled onto the gray carpet and fanned out into a wet, dark circle.

Why did she do it? There had to be a reason. Had she followed him from New York?

No, she wasn't the kind of anonymous sparrow who would have been able to accomplish that. Six feet if she was an inch, and with that wild red hair.

Then she must have something to do with the triptych.

He was breathing heavily, he held a finger to the carotid artery in his neck. It felt engorged, his pulse rate too fast to count. He left the window and sat, closing his eyes.

Jackie LeBeau would find her.

Jackie had arrived from New York via Frankfurt at noon. After a short, intense briefing by Octavian he had set out to locate the bitch. Hanna Anders was her name, they found that out from the desk clerk at the Olympia.

He shouldn't have tried the room roust or the abduction; thanks to that stupid ass Hippolyte things had degenerated into a comic opera farce. The woman had been frightened into checking out of the Olympia.

He hadn't told Jackie the whole story about that. He fumbled for a bottle of blue capsules on the table beside him and downed two.

Forget the bitch. Get his mind on something else.

Jackie. Lately Octavian had begun to suspect he was too dependent on the little man.

He thought back to the time Jackie had appeared at the door of the New York residence six years ago; a fledgling curator from the Metropolitan Museum of Art, who had met Octavian at an exhibition and was cheeky enough to come looking for a job. He had several things going for him besides nerve. He was witty, quite handsome, and well dressed. Best of all, he stood a scant five feet in his thick-soled shoes, against Octavian's five foot six.

It had become routine over the years, Octavian and Jackie meeting for dinner to spend long, cozy hours discussing the intricacies and fine points of Octavian's latest schemes.

For the last three days Jackie had been in Philadelphia trying to dig up some further scrap of information about the location of the triptych. The damned old Anderson hag had been dotty as a

March hare, or pretended to be. She died too easy, almost as if she welcomed the chance.

Octavian had endured three long days and nights without intelligent companionship, made worse by the appearance of that damn redheaded amazon.

There was no real reason to worry about Jackie, he reassured himself. His favorite employee had been offered bribes more than once for information about Octavian; some of those offers Octavian had engineered himself, as tests. Jackie had been too loyal to accept a single one.

Or too smart.

He felt calmer. His breathing had slowed to normal, the pulse in his throat was steady again. He reached for a pink jade box, extracted a pinch of white powder, and sniffed.

The phone rang. He snatched up the receiver.

"Jackie?" He listened for a moment.

"You've found her. Excellent."

Then, in a lowered voice, "Will you be back in time for dinner?"

E·I·G·H·T

VIBRANT rays from the setting sun transformed the prevailing gray stone of Basel's ancient city, playing with warm color harmonies of gold and pink, accented against violet shadows. Hanna returned to the Ange Noir, parked her rental Volkswagen and walked into the lobby.

The room bustled with discreet excitement. Small groups of people chattered as they milled between elevators, the concierge's desk, and the outside door. Anticipation lit up the faces of those who had finished with the day's activities, and now were busy planning a gala evening. Theatre tickets changed hands, Pauli dispensed advice about restaurants and cabarets.

Hanna had two hours to kill before her date with Clete Cross, and she didn't feel like being alone in her room. At the far side of the lobby logs in the fireplace crackled invitingly. She found a vacant chair and abandoned herself to the luxurious embrace of down-filled cushions.

The murmur of conversation was pleasant. Musical voices, the comfortable chair and heat from the fire worked together, making her feel included in society, but not expected to make a contribution.

She thought about the day with pleasure. It seemed to have been a turning point, everything had gone well.

Except, of course, finding out that Madeleine Anderson was dead. She had never met the old woman, but one thing for sure, Madeleine and Dedushka must not have had much in common. Her grandfather had radiated warmth to those he loved, how could his sister have treated him with such implacable indifference?

Conscience reminded her she had received a new piece to the puzzle from Mrs. O'Connor: Madeleine's escalating mental illness. Maybe that was the key to her irrational and sometimes cruel behavior.

Enough of that, there were more pleasant things to think about. Her tour of the Ange Noir, for instance.

Madame Lechard was a born storyteller, who spiced historical information with tales of family and prominent guests over the years. Three hours had melted away before Hanna thought to check the time. She thanked Madame L., collected a map and car keys from Pauli, and wandered through the oldest parts of town until sunset. Yes, it was a good day.

It would be fun to talk with Christian and Malika, now that things were looking up. She wouldn't mention the lost paintings, of course, or yesterday's narrow escape.

Should she tell Malika about meeting an interesting man, and that she was going to dinner with him? No, probably not. Malika would ask how they met, and Hanna had already decided not to bring up the great kidnap caper. In fact, the whole incident was becoming unreal, as if she'd read the book, or seen the movie.

"Is that by any chance a map of Basel?"

Hanna was startled. A handsome, deeply tanned man had materialized from nowhere, like the proverbial ant at a picnic. He stood in front of her with the insouciance of an impudent little boy, sure of his welcome. He had curly black hair and a muscular, well-proportioned body.

He was extremely short.

"Were you dozing? I'm sorry, I know it's rude to disturb you. The thing is, today's Sunday and I can't find a city map for love or money. Is that one I see on your lap?"

He beamed, displaying teeth that would do credit to a toothpaste commercial. He was natty in dark slacks, an impeccably tailored gray jacket, and yellow shirt open at the neck to display an ascot. The effect was that of a thirties matinee idol.

"You do speak English, don't you?" he added, slightly daunted by Hanna's silent stare.

"Yes, I do. The man at the concierge's desk, Pauli, has maps. I'm sure he'd be glad to give you one of your own."

"No one's there right now. Besides, I'm not staying here, I came by for a drink with a friend. Couldn't I just have a peek at yours?"

"I suppose so." No way to refuse without being churlish.

He sat in the chair beside her and reached for the map. Hanna gave it to him. He smoothed the creases and traced two or three routes with an extended finger. Satisfied, he folded the unwieldy paper with precise care, but didn't relinquish it.

"I'm glad you're American. My French is bad and my German unmentionable." His voice gave an odd, coaxing intimacy to the words.

"Why did you single me out? Do I have 'Made in USA' stamped on my forehead?"

"No, but I saw the map and decided you weren't a native. I try English on everybody before I stumble into another language. I'm overjoyed to find a countryman."

"Countryman? Why do you have a British accent?"

"I'm an American citizen, but I've lived abroad most of my life. My father was in the diplomatic service."

"Then I'm surprised you don't speak French. I thought it was the language of diplomacy." Hanna cursed herself for being caught up in conversation. If she'd keep her mouth shut maybe he'd go away.

"Astute of you to pick up on that," he flattered. "Truth is, I never made the effort. I'm not proud of it. Youthful rebellion, I suppose."

This time Hanna did keep her mouth shut. It didn't work, he bestowed another dazzling smile.

"I'm afraid I'm getting off to a bad start with you." He extended a manicured hand. "Jackie LeBeau."

What could she do? Hanna allowed her palm to be clasped and muttered "Hanna Anders."

She was being imposed on and knew it, but he seemed so vulnerable. A jockey-size man trying to impress with a fake accent, spurious diplomatic background, and David Niven costume. Pathetic.

"I've been in town since last Monday. Banking conference," he confided. "Would you believe this is the first time I've had a minute to myself? I've been dying for privacy, and now that I have it I feel at loose ends. Perverse, isn't it?"

Hanna shrugged. "Not uncommon, I expect." She felt a sudden stir of interest. "Banking conference? I met another American banker yesterday. His name is Clete Cross. Do you know him?"

The ingenuous eyes narrowed. "Clete Cross. Name sounds familiar, but . . . no, I can't say I do."

Here it came again. The winsome smile. "Basel's an international banking center, what red-blooded American can resist a junket to Switzerland at company expense? I suspect the woods, or more accurately the hotels, are full of us."

He was lying. Clete's name had evoked more than the normal "let me see, now" reaction. He knew, or knew of, Clete Cross. So why the pretense?

"What are you doing in Basel?" he asked, interrupting her speculation. "On your way to a ski resort?"

"I'm here on business."

"What do you do? Let me guess. You're an airline stewardess," he stated triumphantly.

Wonderful. He thinks he's flattered me.

"I'm an artist," she blurted.

"You're here to paint? What fun. But why Basel? It's an odd location for an artist to select, isn't it?"

"Why does everyone ask that? I have family ties here."

"Oh? Visiting relatives? Smart of you to stay in a hotel. Privacy means a lot, I say."

"I'm not visiting anyone. There's a family legend about something that happened here a long time ago, I was curious to see the place, that's all."

She looked at her watch and composed an "oh, dear, look at the time, I must fly," comment.

He was too quick for her. "Please don't go yet. You can spare a few minutes, can't you? Tell me how this Clete Cross managed an introduction. Clete Cross. The name absolutely rings with macho appeal. I'll bet he had something better than my poor excuse of borrowing your map. Come on, tell. I might learn something."

Hanna's guard relaxed, she couldn't hold back a grin. "As introductions go, his was spectacular. He rescued me from a man who was in the process of dragging me off the street and into his car." As soon as the words were out Hanna regretted them. Why the devil had she told him that?

"You don't mean it! Incredible. Did you know the person? Have you reported it to the police?"

"I didn't know him, and I didn't report it to the police. I was aching and exhausted, the last thing I wanted to do was spend the night in a police station, filling out forms and answering questions.

"Besides, what good would it do? There must be hundreds of black Mercedes sedans in Basel. I didn't get a good look at the man and I don't have time for a lot of official folderol. I'm going to forget the whole thing and get on with my business."

"But where did this Clete Cross come from? How lucky he was around when you needed him. Didn't he suggest calling the police? Maybe he got a license number?"

"We didn't discuss it. I told you, I really mean to put the incident behind me. I'm sorry I mentioned it at all.

"And now I do have to go, I have a dinner engagement. Maybe we'll run into each other again. If not, enjoy your stay."

He leaned so close it was impossible for Hanna to move without shoving him aside.

"With Clete Cross the Valiant, I'll bet. Damn, I was going to ask you out myself. I'd love to see you another time, Hanna Anders. May I phone?"

He leaned back and looked down at himself with a rueful grin. "I'm really quite harmless. But maybe you're embarrassed to be seen with me? Don't feel bad, lots of women are."

Swell. Now a brush-off would seem like a slap at his height. Hanna knew what that felt like, from the other end of the spectrum.

"Of course I wouldn't be embarrassed, it never occurred to me," she lied. "I may be hard to find, but . . . sure, call, if you like. Leave a message at the desk. Maybe we can have a quick cup of coffee one day next week; that is, if you're still here." She stood and held out her hand for the map.

Jackie jumped up and presented it with great ceremony. The top of his head came to her collarbone. Hanna thought of an article she had read once about Mickey Rooney and his tall woman fetish.

"I'll call first thing in the morning. You mentioned a family legend, let me help you track it down. Say you will, please, I love to do things like that. We can have lunch tomorrow and make plans." The wondrous smile threatened to split his face. Really his best effort yet, displaying a whole mouthful of dazzling teeth.

"I'm afraid that's not possible. Some of my paintings were . . . lost, it's put me in a bind for time. When I'm working I don't stop for lunch, it breaks my concentration. I just take something along to nibble on."

"All right, but I'm not giving up. I'll call tomorrow evening."

Hanna forced a tepid grimace and bolted for the elevator.

"I hope Clete Cross, hero, turns out to be a terrible bore," he called after her.

• • •

Jackie watched Hanna disappear, then found a public telephone and dialed.

"Mr. Octavian Demopolis' suite, please." As he waited he hummed, keeping time with a restless forefinger.

I'm just a poor, wayfarin' stranger,
Travelin' through this world alone.

The phone crackled. "Octavian? Jackie. I've found the bitch and talked to her."

Pause.

"Sure I'll be back for dinner, I'm starved. Order fish for me, will you? You know what I like."

Pause.

"Don't worry, I had her purring like a tabby cat. Didn't suspect a thing. Now we know where she's staying, we can get our hands on her anytime.

"Listen, I found out something that'll interest you. Clete Cross is in town, the broad's having dinner with him tonight. Says they just met. Accidentally."

He winced and held the receiver away from his ear.

"Of course Cross is after the triptych, but how in sweet mother hades did he get wind of it? Through the broad?"

He held the receiver out again and waited for the noise to subside.

"No, I didn't find out what her tie-in is, although I have some ideas. What do you expect from a five-minute talk? Listen, let's discuss this over a drink, okay? There're a couple of things I want to ask you about, too."

A rumble of acquiescence came from the receiver.

"I'm on my way. 'Bye."

N·I·N·E

HANNA poked through the contents of her suitcase with disdain. "Looks like something you'd find in a missionary barrel," she muttered.

There were a few warm weather things she'd brought for the visit to Ibiza, hardly suitable for the chill of Switzerland in autumn. Aside from that, nothing very interesting. Finally she picked up a moss green knit skirt and scoop-neck sweater, then poked around in a clump of belts, scarfs, and her small supply of jewelry.

Be resourceful. You're an artist. If Scarlet O'Hara could do it with parlor drapes. . . .

She settled for a gold leather belt, matching sandals, and a heavy neck chain. That would have to do.

She had a leisurely bath, dressed, and was taking final inventory of her reflection in the closet mirror when the phone shrilled. It was Clete.

"Ready. I'll be right down." There was a husky catch to her voice. Then came the old fluttery stomach, the quickened breath, the flushed cheeks.

Why do I feel this way? Clete Cross will never be more to me than a character in an anecdote: "The strangest thing happened to me in Switzerland . . . I was scared out of my wits . . . but then this great-looking man . . ."

Rehearsing the story put things in perspective. By the time the elevator arrived, docked its ponderous glass and crystal bulk and opened to receive her, Clete was neatly classified and stuffed in a pigeonhole. She hoped.

Watch it, girl. Some people exist within an aura of danger, this man has it in spades. Control the situation or it controls you. Want to find out if Clete knows more about you than he should? Throw in something about Madeleine Anderson, see if that gets a reaction.

If what Dedushka said is true, and there is some fabulous inheritance, nobody could know about it.

That's dumb, of course they could. Madeleine probably blabbed it to half of Philadelphia.

Mrs. O'Connor, the woman who answered the phone in Madeleine's apartment. She might be lying, she seemed damned reticent when I mentioned Ilse Bonnard and Switzerland. Come to think of it, she hung up on me.

Anyway, I'm not afraid of Clete Cross. Not physically afraid.

The elevator doors opened, he was waiting to greet her.

"Hi. I'm starved, where are we going for dinner?" she blurted.

He took her arm. "You look wonderful. My God, your hair is red, how could I have missed that?"

"Not red, exactly. Well, maybe you could say red. It was sopping wet when you saw me, that makes it soggy brown." Oh, hell, she was babbling like an adolescent.

He led her to a car and opened the door. "I love red hair. I knew a girl once who had eyes the color of good sherry, and hair to match. I was crazy about her.

"About dinner," he said as he drove, "lots of restaurants are closed on Sunday night. We're going to try a place my landlady suggested, called the Restaurant Safran-Zunft. According to her the food's good, and it's in a neat old building."

"Your landlady, huh? You seem to have made friends all over. How long have you been in Basel?"

She had asked the question before. Would he remember to give the same answer?

"Not long. I get acquainted easily."

They were quiet after that, except for a few consultations about street signs. Finally Clete parked in a dark, cramped passage, with stone walls rising on either side.

They walked a short way to a sprawling, medieval building with elegant proportions. On either side of the entrance were replicas of scholars, crouched slightly above head level. There was a graceful archway topped by a stone fleur-de-lis, and a wrought-iron sign depicting a rotund monk who blissfully contemplated his wine goblet.

Hanna loved it. She backed into the street for a better view of the five-story facade.

Rough arms encircled her, jerked forward. She screamed "No!" and lashed out with flailing arms. The ground vibrated. There was a rumble, lights flashed.

"Hanna, stop it! It's me, Clete." The rumbling subsided, he released her.

"I didn't mean to scare you, but damn it, you were backing into the path of that tram. Another minute and you'd have been under the wheels. I'm beginning to think you need a keeper."

Hanna stalked through the archway, muttering, "Sorry, I should watch where I'm going."

The restaurant was busy, but Clete had called ahead for reservations. They were ushered to a table, menus were presented with a flourish.

Clete ordered wine. He looked at Hanna and began a sentence, then aborted it. He touched her cheek.

"Tears? I'm sorry for that crack about needing a keeper. You were really frightened, weren't you?"

"Leftover nerves, I guess. I'm okay. Did your landlady have any suggestions about what we should order?"

He let her change the subject. "As a matter of fact, she did. They're famous here for their Fondue Bacchus. Veal, with a slew of condiments. Suit you?"

"Sounds great."

In a few minutes they were laughing together at the intricacies of spearing, dipping, and eating the messy, delicious food.

"I love fondue," Clete said. "Part of it's feeling like I'm doing something illicit. Like when I snuck pieces of bread into my mother's stew while it was still simmering on the stove. Hell to pay if she caught me, but it was worth it."

Hanna laughed. "When you're a child, the chance of getting caught adds to the flavor. Where did you grow up, Clete?"

"Sioux Falls, South Dakota."

"Sioux Falls, South Dakota!"

"What's wrong with that?" He dunked another bite of veal.

"Nothing. You just strike me as an urban individual, not a small-town boy from the middle west."

"What do you mean, small town? Sioux Falls is as urban as it gets, in South Dakota."

"I wasn't being condescending, I'm a westerner, too." Hanna felt expansive, full of good food and wine. She sat back and idly twisted the stem of her glass.

"What do people do, in Sioux Falls?"

Clete took it as a question about his own family, which it was.

"My father was owner, publisher, and editor of the daily newspaper. And you were right when you suspected I'm not entirely a midwesterner. Dad died when I was fourteen. Mom sold the paper and we moved to Boston, where she came from."

He polished off the last bite of veal and continued. "She and Dad had met at Harvard. She never liked Sioux Falls; after he died she couldn't get out of there fast enough."

"That must have been hard on you, to lose your father and

move away all at once. Fourteen is a rough age to have your world fall apart."

"It was, but I got over it. Enough of me, let's talk about Hanna Anders. Where did you grow up?"

A nerve quivered in Hanna's throat. She felt so damned attracted to this man, it was difficult to be careful about what she told him.

"Denver, Colorado," she said, feeling her way.

"I'm an only child. Dad traveled a lot, my mother didn't like me much. My grandfather made up for everything, though. He lived with us. When he died, it was the worst thing that's ever happened to me."

"What was he like?"

"Dignified. Some people called him arrogant, but he was very loving to me. He used to tell the most wonderful stories about his childhood. He was Russian, his parents had sent him to America as a boy to escape the threat of revolution. In fact, it's because of him I've come here."

Clete pushed his plate away. "You lost me, what does Basel have to do with your Russian grandfather?" His voice conveyed nothing but polite interest.

Hanna's throat was dry. She sipped water. Was she enmeshed in some kind of deadly game? She tried to read his expression. Nothing. Only the green-gold of his eyes made him seem like a patient, stalking leopard.

Another sip of water. She had to say something.

"He had a younger sister who was brought here by a family friend, a few months after he'd left for the States. She stayed until just before World War II, when Dedushka . . . Grandfather, managed to trace her. He came and took her back to America.

"I thought it would be interesting to have a look at the place where she lived. Talk to some people who knew her, if I'm lucky."

"Would you like dessert? Coffee?" he added, when she shook her head to dessert.

"Coffee sounds good."

Clete signalled the waiter and ordered, then picked up the conversation. "I'd think if you were really interested in family history, you'd go to Russia. Or are you afraid to travel there?"

"It just never appealed to me. At the risk of sounding maudlin, I guess that's because the Russia Dedushka described doesn't exist anymore."

"True. Do you have anything to go on, in Basel? Names or addresses? Did your grandfather's sister leave anything like that?"

"Why do you assume she's dead?"

"You didn't tell me she was? Something in the way you talked about her, I guess. And the time element. Was I mistaken?"

"No, but she only died last week." Hanna kept her voice neutral.

The coffee arrived, providing a diversion. After the waiter was gone Clete came up with a fresh topic. "My landlady had one more suggestion. You may have noticed there's a full moon. She said we should drive to the old Cathedral, the Munster, they call it. I'm sure you've seen the building, it's visible from almost anywhere in town, sitting up on that hill like the queen of the city.

"Anyway, she says it's spectacular in moonlight. Would you like to go?"

Hanna set aside her coffee. "Why not?"

Thirty minutes later they pulled to a stop a few hundred yards from the Cathedral. The view was stunning and they sat enjoying the most comfortable silence of the evening.

Finally Hanna said, "Did I tell you I'm painting inside there tomorrow? I wrote ahead for permission. You have to fill out dozens of forms, and send them back with letters of recommendation. Very complicated, but I'm beginning to believe it was worth it."

There was no indication he'd heard.

"Clete? What are you thinking?"

"Sorry." He picked up her hand, ran his fingers across the back of it. "Something trivial. You'll laugh. I've never gone out with a woman as tall as I am before, it puts me off balance." He sighed. "God, I know you must be sick of hearing about your height."

"You handle it better than most, at least you're straightforward. What I hate are the stupid jokes, meant to cut me down to size. As if I chose to be six feet tall."

"What did you do, keep on growing after the other girls quit?"

"I was five foot nine by the time I was eleven."

"Oh, hell, that was rough."

"You sound as if you know."

"I do, in a way. When I was in the sixth grade, back in Sioux Falls, there were three of us guys who hung out together. Mack Swain, Whitey Krouse, and me.

"Whitey was a farm boy. A quiet, intelligent kid with pale blue eyes and the blondest hair I ever saw, outside of the bottle kind. That's where he got the nickname. Pretty obvious, I guess.

"Well, Whitey went off to wheat harvest with his father the summer before we started junior high. When he left the three of us were pretty much the same size. But on the first day of school that fall there was Whitey, five inches taller than Mack and me. He even had a few straggly whiskers.

"We were jealous as hell until we realized the grownups expected him to act like a man. When we did crazy stuff Mack and I still got off light. After all, we were just little kids. Whitey caught the devil. Poor gawky kid, not even thirteen years old."

"Did you ever see him again, after you moved to Boston?"

"No. The year I graduated from high school I went to Sioux Falls for a visit. Mack and I had kept in touch. We had some good times, that last summer together.

"I asked about Whitey, of course. Mack said he'd gotten in trouble for stealing a truck-load of tires. He was in reform school."

"It's a terrible thing, Clete, the cruelty. Even when it's not deliberate. People can be like a pack of animals who turn against a defective member and kill it. Only humans are more civilized, they just make you miserable.

"I barely remember playing with other children. Couldn't flirt, be kittenish, even cry. I was this big, awkward redhead, in a world full of little girls and boys. One teacher treated me as if I were retarded. She knew I was the same age as everyone else."

Clete put an arm around her. "Those times are over. You're a beautiful woman, you must know that."

"Yes and no. I'm not blind, I can see I'm attractive. Part of the time, anyway. But when I do something dumb or clumsy, I revert to being a kid in a giant's body."

Clete touched her cheek, lifted her hair. "That's silly."

"I know. Maybe I'll outgrow it someday."

"Start now. Look at me."

She raised her head. The kiss began with familiar tentative seeking; lips, tongue, is this what pleases you, or this? His hand stroked her neck, the back of her head. Gentle fingers found the swell of a breast, the delicate slant of her rib cage, then moved to follow the curve of her waist. Hip, thigh, and inner leg felt his gentle, insistent caress. The age-old, tantalizing question loomed. Should I? Shouldn't I? The decision was taken away from Hanna.

His withdrawal was something sensed, at first. An awareness that the spirit of the man no longer inhabited the flesh that touched hers. Hanna tensed, her eyes opened. His mouth and hands left her, slowly but with resolution.

He chuckled. "Look, the windows are all steamed up.

"I'd better get you back to the hotel," he added into chilly silence.

At the Ange Noir he pulled to the curb and stopped without cutting the engine. "I'll see you to your room." A perfunctory offer.

Hanna was already out. "Don't bother. Thanks for dinner."

"Later, then? How about lunch tomorrow?"

"I'll be at the Cathedral. I don't eat when I'm working." Hadn't she been through this conversation before?

"I'll drop by for a visit. May I watch you paint, if I'm quiet?"

"I don't like an audience."

She couldn't leave it like that. "Come in the middle of the afternoon, I'll be ready for a break."

"See you tomorrow, then."

• • •

Hanna crawled into bed and pulled the comforter up to her ears. Her mind raced. Tense nerves, taut muscles, pulled her into a hard, unyielding knot of misery. She was so damn confused. And cold. Colder than she had ever been in her life. She called forth the image of Ibiza's beach. Sun, water, crystal grains of sand frosting her arms and legs. Heat radiating from the beach, the sea . . .

It worked. She unwound, feeling the warmth suffuse her body. In Scarlet's incomparable fashion, she would worry about her problems tomorrow.

T·E·N

CLETE drove to the Leopard as fast as he could maneuver through narrow, twisted streets. In thirty minutes Frank would begin his watch at the Ange Noir; Clete had to see him first.

It was near Sunday closing, only a few stragglers remained inside the bar. Frank sat at a table near the door. Marga caught Clete before he could get there.

"I am ready to go home in a few minutes. You did not come last night."

"Sorry, *Liebchen*. I had to work."

"Work. You were with that English cow you brought here. Big, wet bitch."

"She's American. Bring me some beer, will you, love?" Clete watched her leave, her beautiful body swaying seductively. Too bad. There wouldn't be time for that tonight, either.

"How'd it go?" Frank asked.

Clete shrugged. "Okay, I guess. She mentioned the Anderson woman. Hanna's great-aunt, according to her."

"Did she say anything about the triptych?"

"No, she's too smart for that. Sometimes I felt like she was baiting me, watching for a reaction. I did slip up once."

"How?"

"Took it for granted Madeleine Anderson was dead. She called me on it. I put it back on her, and said she'd given me that impression."

"Was she satisfied?"

"Hard to tell. She puts on a brave show, but she's jittery as a prostitute in a prayer meeting."

"She ought to be. Sounds to me like she's playing us, or you, against Octavian. Did she say anything more about being attacked last night?"

"No, come to think of it."

"Isn't that odd? She must not have called the police, either."

Clete rubbed the stubble on his chin. "You're right, or I'd have heard about it. She'd have to give my name as a witness. Well, you can't figure women. Maybe she was scared to call the cops in a foreign country. She doesn't speak German or French, beyond a few tourist phrases."

"Or maybe she has good reason not to attract the attention of the local constabulary."

"Yeah, you could be right. Enough of her, tell me about you. Find anything interesting on Stillestrasse?"

Frank turned his palms up. "Depends on how you look at it. The street twists and turns through the old town. Mile and a half long, roughly. Narrow row houses on one end, well kept, some of them with business on the first floor. You know the kind.

"Then you cross a small park with a statue of some local hero, and on the other side are virtual palaces. Walls, grounds, the works. Discreet brass plaques on places that have gone to business; one a private research institute of some kind, the other a girls' school. Or had been, it didn't have the feel of a going concern."

"Talk to anyone?"

"Yeah, on the row house end. No one knew or remembered

any Bonnards. I couldn't get anybody to open up on the snooty side."

"Figures," Clete grunted. "I don't think it will matter. Hanna Anders, if that's her name, will lead us to the triptych."

"If Octavian doesn't get her first."

"Yeah." Clete downed the last of his beer. "And speaking of that, you'd better be off to guard the golden goose. Or maybe she's a Trojan horse?"

Frank grunted.

"Anyway," Clete continued, "only the main entrance of the Ange Noir is open after eight P.M. There's an attendant at the front desk all night. She's probably safe as a babe in its mother's arms as long as she's inside. Nevertheless . . ."

"Yeah, who can tell about Octavian? Seems to me he's getting damn reckless."

• • •

"How could you be so goddam reckless?" Jackie LeBeau's voice was raised in complaint. He was scared, which made him forget to be diplomatic.

"That was a fool thing, turning Hippo loose on the girl. You don't just kidnap people off the street and get by with it. Not in Switzerland. This isn't Calcutta, goddammit."

Octavian played with a pink quartz snuff box, his fingers caressing the cool, slippery surface. He hadn't seen fit to tell Jackie about the embarrassment of the botched kidnapping. Hanna Anders' description of dramatic rescue was unfortunate.

In retrospect, Jackie was right. He made a mild response to the tirade.

"It could have worked."

"My ass." Jackie was off again. "Damn it, there was no need for that. You were in the car yourself, I bet. Well, were you?"

Octavian nodded curtly.

"Insanity. What if the police had caught you? What if there'd been a witness who made note of the license?" Jackie was turned on by his own rhetoric. Preparing another salvo, he glowered at Octavian.

He'd gone too far. A shiver ran down his spine, he put out a placating hand.

"I'm sorry, that was out of line. It's just that I worry about you, you know that." He sat on the floor beside Octavian's chair, allowed his eyes to soften. An impudent grin curved his lips.

"If anything happened to you, what would become of me?"

E·L·E·V·E·N

FRANK took a last drag and jammed his cigarette into the ashtray. It overflowed, stale butts spilled out onto the floor mat. Frank ignored them. He stretched and rubbed his eyes.

Gray dawn had smudged the sharp edge of darkness. He squinted, tried to read his watch. Too much light for the luminous dial, too dark to see without it. He switched on the map light. Seven A.M. Clete would relieve him at nine, they had agreed Hanna wouldn't stir before then.

Two hours. Frank imagined himself showering and easing between fresh sheets, sinking deep in the feather bed. Ah, paradise!

Bundled in thermal underwear, sweat suit, insulated parka and gloves, he was still cold as a well digger's rear end.

And sleepy. God, he was sleepy. His eyelids drooped, soothing numbness spread through his arms and legs. He floated, shedding his body like a cicada.

A muscle spasm stabbed him in the neck. "Hell!" He massaged with cautious fingers, making a random excursion into his repertoire of profanity.

Dawn was coming fast. Hanna's blue Volks was clearly visible, even to a rusty dent in the right rear fender. Frank poured the last drops of coffee from his thermos and swallowed. His empty stomach rumbled in protest.

Eight-forty, only a few minutes to go. He looked up and down the street.

There were worse things than being sleepy. His bladder reminded him of one.

Two boys approached; slender, moving with the self-conscious bravado of street punks. One had purple and orange hair, he wore a black leather jacket and silver lamé pants; his friend was resplendent in day-glo orange and peacock. They were heavily made up, each flaunted a single gold earring shaped like a scimitar.

They passed the Peugeot and saw Frank. Orange-purple hair blew him a kiss. Frank stared straight ahead. Last thing he needed was a rumble.

An engine sputtered to life, the Volks began to move.

"Sonofabitch!" He'd been watching the boys, hadn't seen her come out. He jabbed the starter, nosed the Peugeot into the street.

"Figures," he muttered. "Damned amazon, shoulda known you wouldn't sleep in like a normal broad."

The Volks slid into a right-hand turn.

Frank whistled. "What's this? Not going to the Cathedral? You lost, or something? Don't tell me you didn't bring your Girl Scout compass."

She was driving fast, not the hesitant crawl of a muddled tourist. The Volks turned again. Frank's brain sounded an alert.

"Bingo! Stillestrasse."

Hanna slowed. They were at the blue-blood end of the street. She lingered at the entrance of one mansion, then moved on to another. At the second she parked and got out, studied the engraved brass plate and then disappeared into the entry.

The defunct girls' school. Frank backed up a discreet two hundred feet and cut his engine, partially concealed by overhanging shrubs. He was wide awake now.

Knew exactly where you were going, didn't you, baby? Bring the triptych out like a good girl, Papa'll take it off your hands. Clete and me can get the hell out of here with the jackpot and our hides in one piece, before Octavian knows his ass from a hole in the ground.

Five minutes passed, ten, twenty. Something had told him it wouldn't be that easy. He thought about Clete, they'd just missed the switch-off. Clete would head for the Cathedral, figuring to catch up there.

Sorry, buddy, you'll just have to stew awhile.

Damn, he needed to pee. He stretched out in the seat and wished he'd brought an empty jar.

He looked at the thermos.

No, better not.

T·W·E·L·V·E

HANNA clanged the heavy bronze stag's head against its rest and waited. The bulk and magnificence of Tante Sophia's made her aware that it was a mistake to have come in work clothes. Why hadn't she dressed for a social call, then gone back to the Ange Noir and changed, before going to the Cathedral? She took a resolute breath. Too late now.

Minutes passed. She banged the knocker again and cinched up her sheepskin coat. It hung to midcalf, eighteen inches of faded Levi's showed between the hem and her leather aerobics shoes.

The skin on the back of her neck prickled; she squirmed. Someone inside that pile of stone was watching her, deciding whether or not to open the door.

Why not just leave? Get in the car, drive away, forget the whole thing. This was humiliating, standing on the doorstep like a beggar at a palace.

A miracle happened. The towering beamed door that looked as immovable as the rock of ages creaked open.

"Mademoiselle Anders?"

"Yes, I'm Hanna Anders."

"Come in."

Hanna walked into an open, vaulted room whose ceiling floated somewhere up with the angels, in dim half light. There was an odor of damp stone, and something else. Her nose wrinkled slightly. An herb? Lavender?

She could see two people, the woman who had let her in and a uniformed girl at the end of a long corridor. The girl disappeared as the woman beside her spoke.

"I am Madame Mercier."

"It's very considerate of you to see me. I'll try not to impose. . . ."

"Please come with me," Madame Mercier cut Hanna off in midsentence. "We will talk in my sitting room, it is quite pleasant there. I have asked Cici to bring coffee."

Madame Mercier was slender, of average height. She walked with the flawless posture of a woman who has been trained to do so without giving it a thought. Her long, elegant neck supported a narrow head, with a nimbus of curly hair that was soft gold mixed with silver.

She led the way into a room of pale yellow silk and ornate, white plaster frescoes. A fire crackled behind a screen encrusted with gilt rosettes. Hanna walked toward it and held out her hands. Madame Mercier joined her.

"Are you chilled? That is why I did not offer to take your coat. It is impossible to heat all this house, we settle for pockets of warmth. Even in summer it is cold, our school girls used to remark on it. We told them it builds character.

"Will you sit here?" She indicated one of a pair of gilt and tapestry chairs beside the fire.

Hanna guessed her age at fifty plus, maybe even sixty. Her skin was almond and smooth, with fine networks of wrinkles around mouth and eyes. Her features were marvelous; narrow, sculptured nose, delicate mouth and chin, glowing, pale green eyes. In short, she was Hanna's idea of the perfect aristocrat.

"So you are Madeleine's great-niece. Tell me about yourself,

Mademoiselle Anders. Do you live close to Madeleine, in Philadelphia? And how is she?"

"I guess you couldn't have known, either. Madeleine's dead, she died last week. I don't want to mislead you; she and I were related, but we never met."

Madame Mercier frowned. "Madeleine's death does not startle me. After all . . . the years go by. But if you were not acquainted, I do not understand your interest in her."

Groping for a way to explain, Hanna was overjoyed by the entrance of the young woman whom she had seen in the hallway. The girl had glossy black hair and a gamine face, and she struggled under the burden of a heavy-laden tray.

"Thank you, Cici. There on the table, please."

To Hanna's surprise Madame Mercier had spoken in English. Cici gave Hanna a quick, warm smile, set down her burden and left.

"Cici has an American boyfriend, she is working very hard to become fluent in his language," Madame Mercier said as she served coffee and small cut-glass tumblers of orange juice.

Hanna slipped her arms out of the sheepskin coat. She accepted coffee, a croissant, and a spoonful of raspberry jam.

Madame Mercier's interrogation was suspended while they ate, conversation consisted of polite chatter about Switzerland's breathtaking landscape.

When they finished the elegant woman put aside her cup, patted her lips, and gave Hanna an expectant look. The amenities had been observed.

"Before I ask for information, I'm sure you'd like proof of my identity." Hanna removed the sapphire ring and offered it for inspection.

After a moment's hesitation Madame Mercier extended a flat palm to receive the ring. She held it at arm's length, then with an exclamation of irritation picked up silver-rimmed glasses and put them on. She brought the ring close to her face and examined it.

"I recognize the crest. It is that of the Romanovs, certainly. Where did you get it?"

"From Dedushka. My grandfather. It's the only thing I have that belonged to him."

"Your grandfather. Madeleine's brother? And are you all that is left of the family, or are your parents alive? Do you have brothers or sisters?"

"I'm an only child. My parents died several years ago in . . . an accident."

Madame Mercier returned the ring and set aside her glasses. "You said you have questions?"

"So many, I hardly know where to begin. First, you said the Romanovs? Weren't they the royal family of Russia? Why would my grandfather have a ring with their insignia on it?"

"You really do not know? Your great-grandfather was a cousin to the Tsar."

Hanna was astounded. "It can't be. Dedushka would have told me . . . how could he not have told me a thing like that?"

"I do not know, of course, but I can make a guess. In the twenties and thirties there were many Russian aristocrats in Europe and America, both real and counterfeit. They were quite sought after socially in your country, I believe.

"But the Bolsheviks were everywhere, so those who were related to the assassinated Tsar mostly kept their own council and prayed they wouldn't be recognized. Your grandfather must have found the habit of silence hard to break."

Madame Mercier poured herself more of the strong coffee and looked inquiringly at Hanna's cup. Hanna shook her head.

"No thanks. Can you tell me more about my great-grandparents?"

"Your great-grandfather was, as I told you, a cousin to Tsar Nicholas. They were close friends as well as kinsmen. His given name was Peter, Tante Ilse called him Petra. He was very handsome, she told me.

"He married Ilse's friend, a charming and elegant Frenchwoman from an impoverished family. That did not matter, he was immensely wealthy himself."

Hanna wasn't sure the whole thing wasn't a fairly tale. She looked down at her worn Levi's and sneakers. Could her hostess be making fun of her for some obscure reason?

"I still can't believe Dedushka wouldn't have told me. The Revolution was ages ago, and besides he knew I'd respect anything he said in confidence.

"It would have sounded so improbable, though." She mused. "Maybe he thought even I wouldn't believe him."

"That might explain why he did not fully confide in you, but I think it more likely apprehension kept him silent for so many years. You have no idea how fearful the émigrés of royal birth were."

"Surely they were safe in America."

"Perhaps."

"Your Tante Ilse. You said she was a friend of my great-grandmother, the Frenchwoman?"

"Lisanne. Yes, they were educated together. Lisanne was a student in this school."

"My great-grandmother lived here, too?" This was new information.

"Yes. It was all so long ago." Madame Mercier seemed restless. She glanced at a clock on the mantel; a frivolous thing with pink enamel flowers and gilt cherubs. It chimed, she shifted in her chair.

She wants to be rid of me. It's these wretched clothes, Hanna thought. She blurted, "Do you remember Madeleine? Did you ever meet my grandfather? Do you have any idea what brought on the estrangement between them?"

"By the time I was old enough to have a memory, Madeleine had been here many years. She taught a few classes, helped Papa and Tante Ilse run the school. She was part of the family.

"I met your grandfather when he came and took her to the

United States, just before World War II. I was still very young.

"As I remember, he was tall and thin, with black curly hair and a solemn face. He gave Madeleine orders, expected her to do as he said.

"They did quarrel. She did not wish to leave Basel, he was adamant. In the end, of course, he prevailed. We were sad to see her go. Especially Tante Ilse.

"And now, Miss Anders, I do not wish to appear ungracious, but I have another engagement. That is really all I can tell you. It happened so long ago, when I was a child. There are no longer traces of Madeleine Anderson here." Madame Mercier stood.

I can't let her do this, Hanna thought. She got out of her chair and stood defiantly with her back to the fire.

"Dedushka said there was a package left with your Aunt Ilse for safekeeping, when he brought his sister to the States. Do you know anything about it?"

Madame Mercier's face flattened into a mask, only her eyes showed a spark of response.

"I know of nothing like that. Do you not think if a box had been left, it would have been shipped to Madeleine as soon as the war was over?"

"Dedushka said not. He said they had agreed it was to be kept here, until a family member came in person for it."

Madame gestured impatiently. "Then you must be more specific. What sort of box, how big? What was in it? I really have no idea what you are talking about.

"Also, if Madeleine and her brother were estranged, as you say, how can he have been sure the box was never sent?"

Hanna swallowed an angry accusation. The woman had said "box, what sort of box?" Hanna herself had spoken of "a package."

"Dedushka was quite positive about the arrangement."

Madame did not intend to put up with any further delay. She walked to the door and turned with a gallic shrug.

"Then it is a mystery, *n'est-ce pas?*"

There was no choice but to follow. As they walked the cold hallway Hanna thought of a safe question.

"Madame Mercier, my great-grandparents; were they killed in the Revolution?"

"I believe so, that is what Tante Ilse said."

They had arrived at the entrance. Madame Mercier faced Hanna with an appraising stare. Hanna didn't flinch.

"Will you be in Basel long?"

"I'm not sure. Several days, at least."

"Where are you staying?"

"The Hotel Ange Noir."

"The Ange Noir. I know it, I have an acquaintance with Madame Lechard, the wife of the proprietor."

"I've met her, she's a very warm person. She asked me to give you her regards."

"Is that so?" Hanna thought she could detect a slight softening, a flicker of interest.

"Perhaps you and I could have afternoon coffee before you leave. May I telephone?"

"Please do. If I'm not in, you can leave a message."

"I will do so. Good-bye, Mademoiselle Anders."

• • •

On the way to the Cathedral, Hanna blamed herself for handling the interview badly. In retrospect, it was inexcusable not to do her hostess the courtesy of proper dress.

Off on the wrong foot, and downhill from there. Was she serious about seeing me again? She did defrost a little when Madame Lechard was mentioned.

How long should I wait before I try something else?

What else?

Would a woman rich and proper as Madame Mercier lie to me in order to keep something that doesn't belong to her?

Depends on what it is, maybe.

Package, box. Her English is flawless, but that's not much of a mistake. Maybe she's telling the truth and never heard of it.

In a pig's eye, she hasn't.

T·H·I·R·T·E·E·N

HANNA had stopped feeling guilty and worked herself into a fine fury by the time she arrived at the Cathedral. She yanked her equipment out of the Volks and carried it inside. Madame Mercier, the Crown Princess of Tante Sophia's, was clearly not telling everything she knew. Maybe her highness could even shed light on the attack against Hanna Saturday night.

She set her easel and canvas bag down with a thump. Paranoia grew. She, Hanna Anders, was the one in danger, but nobody saw fit to tell her a damn thing. Who knew, the Grande Dame might have had a hand in the kidnap attempt herself.

Resigned to a few minutes of inactivity while she waited for her eyes to adjust to inside light, she plopped down on a bench. Her body was an articulated mass of tension. Somehow, by coaxing or coercion, she intended to find out what was going on before. . . .

Before what? What's wrong with me, I'm thinking like an idiot. Madame Mercier was courteous to receive me at all. I'm a stranger, she doesn't owe me a thing.

Unless she has my inheritance.

How likely is it some great fortune has been gathering dust in Ilse Bonnard's attic for sixty years? Grant the improbable, say that it has. Well-bred school mistresses don't arrange abductions. Simmer down, get your mind on your business. You're here to work, remember?

She couldn't sit still. Leaving her equipment under the bench, she explored; remembering the research she'd done on the Cathedral, or more properly, Munster.

The original structure had been consecrated early in the eleventh century, then destroyed by an earthquake. Rebuilt along Romanesque and Gothic lines, it sat on the hilltop with regal dignity, its green and yellow tile roof a whimsical incongruity to her American eyes.

Hanna had always felt an affinity with ancient places. She began to relax. Delicate vibrations from centuries of prayer, supplication, exaltation, moved through the air like an electric current.

She stopped in front of a stone memorial slab that read:

ERASMUS
1536

What did she know about Erasmus? She remembered reading that he was one of the beacons of pure intellect that shine across centuries, like Aristotle and Da Vinci. She had seen a portrait of him by Hans Holbein, the Younger, displaying the chiaroscuro profile of a thin, ascetic face. Eyes cast down in humility. The mouth. . . .

A strident, authoritative tour guide with an obedient herd of tourists intruded, grinding out facts and statistics. Hanna walked back to the bench and retrieved her equipment.

Unfolding the portable easel, she wondered what Erasmus, the great humanist, would make of the officious tour guide, who had just defined Erasmus' existence by spewing out dates and reeling off names of kings and princes who had been his intimates. Different minds, different concepts of reality.

Her own truths might be someone else's fantasies. Were there any absolute verities at all? She wasn't sure.

Clete Cross. What did she believe about him?

She couldn't trust him.

Oh, but she wanted to, wanted to convince herself his illogical behavior had a logical explanation. She was so damned vulnerable where he was concerned. Why? Why this man, above all others? Who was he? Not the banker he claimed to be. She couldn't swallow that.

Her life seemed to be out of her control. She felt like a participant in a masquerade, a player who stood alone, her naked face exposed. She wasn't the world's most stable person. Had she lost the ability to judge what was real?

She squeezed a thick blob of titanium white onto the center of her palette and arranged other colors around it, cool to warm.

What about Jackie LeBeau? She couldn't shake off the idea that their meeting wasn't accidental. The more she thought, the surer she was that he had sought out Hanna Anders, not just someone from whom he could mooch a map.

She began sketching on toned canvas with a fat stick of charcoal. Her work never failed her, it was the one truth that defined her existence. After the first tentative strokes she became an artist, and nothing more.

• • •

"Have time for a break?"

Hanna flinched, her brush slashed a path of burnt umber.

"Damn, Clete. Do you always sneak up on people?"

"I'm sorry." He walked closer and saw the brown slash bisecting the canvas.

"Oh, hell, I *am* sorry. Can you fix it?"

"Yes, it's not a big deal at this stage. Had I been further along, I'd attack you with a palette knife."

"I'll keep that in mind. Stop awhile, talk to me?"

Hanna dropped her brush in the jar of cleaner. "All right. But let's go outside, I'm tired of smelling turpentine and the dust of ages."

"Put your coat on. The wind's come up."

They walked out into the double cloister that opened onto Rittergasse. Clete took her hand."

"Look down there, Hanna, at the city. I take back what I said about Basel. It is beautiful."

She nodded. "A river city. All the wonderful old ones are. When you said what you did about someplace 'more picturesque'—"

"Did I say that?" he interrupted.

"Something like it. Anyway, I couldn't paint some postcard alpine village, the kind you see in magazines, where the jet-setters go to ski. Basel has a soul. People live and die here, it's not a stage set for entertainment."

"I see what you mean.

"Hanna, when you look down, do you feel how old this place is? From up here you can imagine. . . ."

"That if we tried, we could call up the eleventh century, or the fourteenth, or . . . whenever?"

"That's it. There's some kind of theory, isn't there, that time doesn't exist? Everything that's ever happened, or ever will, is taking place right now in a different dimension."

"Yes, I've heard that. Sometimes it seems to me there's only the thinnest membrane, if you could step through it, you'd be, oh, wherever you wanted. In any century you wanted."

What am I babbling about? I've never said that sort of thing to a man before. He started it, though. What a baffling contradiction you are, Clete Cross.

He touched her, she moved easily into his arms. He looked as if he expected answers to be written in the depths of her eyes, on the planes of her face; then he kissed her. The wind moaned.

Hanna began to shiver, not entirely with cold. Clete pulled his coat over her shoulders and said, "You're freezing, nature lover. Let's go inside." He hurried her through the cloister.

Hanna remembered something Clete had told her the night before. "Clete, it's only a few minutes past eleven. You said you had business meetings all morning."

"I skipped out early. Couldn't get you off my mind, beautiful lady, so I gave up trying. Have you been thinking about me?"

Hanna couldn't believe it. Mention business and the sensitive, perceptive man was replaced by a common oaf with a slick line. It made her furious and she lashed out at him.

"Stop it, Clete. Don't insult my intelligence. That kind of fatuous drivel is unworthy of you. Why can't you be honest? What are you doing in Basel, and how does it concern me?"

"I don't know what you're talking about." False, flat voice.

"Then there's nothing more to be said." Hanna picked up a number seven bristle and scrubbed at the canvas with short, violent strokes.

Clete took the brush out of her hand. She glared. He gripped her shoulders, tried to pull her close.

Hanna stiffened, hands clenched at her sides, legs braced. "Stop it!"

He backed away. "Is this one of the times you're a kid in a grownup's body?"

"That's a cheap shot."

"Yes, I guess it was. You're in no mood for company. I'll be in touch later."

Hanna watched him leave, her jaws clenched with frustration.

Clete walked to a narrow, hole-in-the-wall café, sat at the counter, and ordered black coffee. He was supposed to be standing watch, but Hanna wasn't going anywhere for the moment. She was too wrapped up in paint and canvas.

He'd seen a different woman this morning. Self-confident, with the quiet authority of a person who knows what she's doing and is good at it.

He compressed his lips. Damn it, he was thinking of her as a real person again, instead of a job-related problem. It had started when they shared experiences the night before, about people who didn't fit the norm.

She's conning my socks off. She's after the triptych like the rest of us. Hell of a woman, but that doesn't change anything, we're adversaries. Get smart. Keep it that way.

I'm acting like a two-bit gigolo, working to make her fall for me.

So? Part of the game.

Why not be honest? Tell her what I know about the triptych, give her a chance to explain.

What kind of a fool idea is that? You can't stand the stakes, you don't play.

She's an amateur. Maybe she doesn't know the stakes.

So she gets hurt. The world's full of casualties.

He pushed aside the full coffee cup, threw down some change, and walked out.

F·O·U·R·T·E·E·N

HANNA swirled her dirty brushes in turp the color of Mississippi mud, until the last vestiges of burnt umber were sucked from the bristles. She wiped them and put them away in the French easel box.

It had become impossible to paint, the outside light that had been filtering through prismed glass windows all day was gone. She flexed her shoulder muscles and dug knuckles into her eyes.

Tendons in her neck were ropes of fire, she looked down and rolled her head from side to side. There was a bad taste in her mouth; her eyes were gritty with strain. She checked the time. Five-thirty.

As she finished packing and folding the easel she felt light-headed. There'd been nothing for lunch, her only meal had been the croissant at Madame Mercier's. Her body craved dinner, bed, and a good night's sleep. She secured the wet canvas in its brackets and pulled on her coat.

A blast of icy wind buffeted her as she left the building, forcing an involuntary gasp. She was disoriented in the restless dark. Where had she left the Volks?

There were quite a few cars still in the parking area, whose owners must be swallowed up somewhere inside the Munster. The full moon, cold and distant, was partially veiled by fast-moving plumes of cloud. Hanna shuddered and walked faster.

Locating the car hidden behind an old Volvo, she unlocked the passenger door and put in her equipment. As she walked around to the driver's side an engine started close by.

The sound startled her. She hurried into the Volks and locked the doors, then jammed her key in the starter and twisted. After an initial hiccup the motor purred with reassuring efficiency.

She let it idle a minute, then flipped on headlights and looked around.

No other lights, no movement, no sound above the cheerful perk of the Volks engine. She pulled away and started down the hill. Suddenly lights blazed in her rearview mirror, a car followed out of the parking area.

Nothing to worry about. Just another Cathedral visitor going home. Still, fear made an acid lump in her throat. Was it a black Mercedes?

Impossible to tell. She swerved around a corner, the car stayed with her. She made another turn, and another, onto a crowded main street where she became an anonymous part of the stream. No way to know if the car from the Cathedral was still with her.

There was a parking space close to the door of the Ange Noir, she pulled in, grabbed her things, and ran.

Safety. Lights, warmth, people.

"Hanna! There you are. I was about to give up waiting and have a lonesome drink—my God, is something the matter? You look like the Hounds of Hell are after you." Jackie LeBeau, resplendent in a fawn jacket and chocolate trousers, cocked his head up at her and made noises of concern.

She didn't want to cope with him now, damn it. "What are you doing here, Jackie?"

"I thought. . . ." He hesitated.

"I don't mean to be rude; but I've been working all day, I'm grungy, and I haven't eaten since morning. You should have called."

Making a visible effort to hang onto his aplomb, Jackie turned on the high wattage smile. "Don't be mad. I have something exciting to tell you. Come sit down a few minutes. Please?"

Tired as she was, it seemed less trouble to comply than refuse. Hanna stalked to a chair and sat on the edge.

"Well, what is it?"

"First let me take care of these things." He picked up her easel and carry-all.

"Be careful, that canvas is wet."

"Yes, ma'am." He carried her things to the concierge's desk and handed them to Pauli. She saw money change hands, her things were stowed behind the desk.

"He'll take them to your room himself, as soon as he has a chance," Jackie said, sitting in the chair beside her.

"Look, you haven't eaten, you said so. Come have one quick drink and dinner with me. I'll tell my news, then off to bed with you. Poor baby, you do look beat."

She was hungry. "Okay. But here in the hotel, and only one drink, I'm holding you to that."

He took her arm. She bent awkwardly in an attempt to minimize the differences in their sizes, feeling like a horse being led by a determined jockey.

At the table he ordered two martinis. He reached for her hand, she put it in her lap. He ignored the rebuff.

"You looked scared to death when you came in. What spooked you?"

"Nothing, I spooked myself. I'm still jittery from that business Saturday evening. I told you about it. Can we drop the subject?"

The drinks were served. Hanna sipped, wishing she'd been firmer and gotten rid of him. Now she was stuck through dinner.

"You said you have something to tell me," she prompted. What could he possibly know that he believed she would find exciting?

"First let's order, then we can talk undisturbed."

"Sounds good to me." Maybe he was going to keep his word about a quick meal.

He summoned the waiter, consultations were held, and the man left. Jackie leaned forward with a conspiratorial air.

"My conferences hit a snag today. Nobody could agree on anything, we're taking a couple of days to cool off and check with home offices. I have some free time, and I'm in the mood for fun."

I don't think I want to know what your idea of fun is, little man.

Jackie drained his glass as the waiter arrived with fresh drinks.

Better nip this in the bud. "I don't want another martini, just food."

With a sympathetic glance at Jackie, the server removed her glass.

Waiter thinks I'm a bitch. Well, I don't care.

Jackie hurried into conversation. "Remember telling me about connections you have in Basel, some kind of family legend? It sounded fascinating. I'm a good research man. What do you say, let's explore together, run down your mystery. We can make an adventure of it."

"There's no mystery, I didn't realize I gave you that impression. And I don't have time to sightsee, I need to finish the painting I started in the Cathedral and move on. I told you, some of my works have disappeared. I can't afford to waste time."

"A couple of days off won't hurt anything. Please? No strings attached, Hanna, I swear not to make a pass at you."

Fascinating. He was begging like an infatuated fool, but his eyes were narrow slits of dislike. Why the charade? Could she push hard enough to shake his control, find out what he was up to?

She yawned elaborately and stared past Jackie's head. There was a mirror on the wall, through it she could see the lobby entrance to the dining room. She stopped breathing. Clete Cross stood in the doorway, making frantic signals. She bounded out of her chair, bumping the table as she went.

"Jackie, you'll have to excuse me a minute."

"All right, but you're not getting off the hook. I want a favorable reply when you get back."

She hurried to the lobby. No sign of Clete. Had she been hallucinating?

In no hurry to return to the dining room, she went to the desk to check for messages. The young woman on duty had been introduced earlier as Madame Lechard's niece.

"Good evening, Sylvie. Is there anything in my box?"

"I believe there is, Mademoiselle. I remember . . . yes, here it is." She handed over a monogrammed envelope.

Hanna tore it open and admired the strong, elegant handwriting a moment before she read:

> Mademoiselle Anders,
>
> I ask your pardon for dismissing you this morning. I needed time to think.
>
> Would it be possible for you to return this evening, and be my guest for a day or two? I think you will find it interesting.
>
> If I do not hear otherwise, I will expect you between seven and eight o'clock.
>
> Helene Mercier

Hanna shoved the note in her pocket and headed for the elevator in panic. What time was it now?

"Ssst! Hanna. Over here." Clete, motioning from the mouth of a service hall.

Hanna walked closer, eyeing him with suspicion. "What are we playing, *I Spy*?"

He ignored the jibe, countering with a question of his own. "What are you doing with LeBeau?"

"So you do know each other. Swell. You have dinner with him, I'm going to my room."

"Hanna, that little charmer is deadly. I don't have time to explain. Pack your things while I keep an eye on him, I'm going to get you out of here."

Hanna stifled a flippant remark. Maybe she could play the men against each other while she got away to Madame Mercier's. It was worth a try.

Clete grabbed her arm. Urgency crackled through his fingers.

"Hanna, please do as I ask. Once you're safe I'll tell you anything you want to know. I need some straight answers from you, too."

"I don't know what you mean by that. Oh, all right."

He reconnoitered the lobby, then hurried her to the elevator. "I'll call you in five minutes. Be ready."

"Ten."

"Ten, but not a minute more, damn it." The elevator opened, he gave her a little push. "Go!"

As the doors closed he whispered, "Ten minutes, not a second longer."

Inside her room Hanna dialed the front desk. "Sylvie? Hanna Anders. Is Madame Lechard in her flat?"

"I believe so, Mademoiselle, do you wish me to ring her?"

"Please."

Hanna held her breath as she counted the double rings, two . . . three . . .

"Oui? Madame Lechard ici."

"Madame, this is Hanna Anders. I've been invited to stay a night or two with Madame Mercier. I want to keep my room here, of course, but I need to leave right away."

"Oh? That is nice. Is there some way I can be of assistance?"

"I have a very embarrassing problem. There are two gentlemen in the lobby, both have asked me to dinner. I'd like to get out of the hotel without seeing either of them. Is that possible?"

A short, surprised "oh" was followed by a laugh.

"You young people. You may leave through this flat, we have

a private entrance. Come to the back hall, down the stairway to the second floor. I will be waiting for you."

"Oh, thanks! I'll be there in"—she looked at her watch—"five minutes. Should I ask Sylvie to call a taxi?"

"It is not necessary, I will be pleased to drive you."

"You're an angel, Madame Lechard."

In frantic haste Hanna stuffed clothes into a small, collapsible case and washed her hands and face. There was no time to change clothes. "Here I come in my Levi's again, Madame Mercier," she said with regret.

The phone shrilled as she closed the door and ran to the back stairs.

So long, Clete. You and Jackie probably deserve one another.

F·I·F·T·E·E·N

MADAME Lechard chattered happily on the drive to number 23 Stillestrasse, while Hanna gave absent-minded answers. Her mood swung between elation at having pulled off an escape under the noses of both men, and guilt for deliberately misleading Clete. The ringing phone echoed in her ears, she imagined Clete puzzled, Clete anxious, Clete furious, Clete crossed; and giggled to herself.

She shouldn't have run out on him like that, there was hardly a shred of proof that he was anything but what he claimed to be. Maybe all her suspicions were neurotic imaginings. Which left her running away from a man to whom she was extremely attracted, a man who had saved her life.

I'll telephone him later from Madame Mercier's.

How? He didn't tell me where he was staying, just mentioned "a small pension." I'll never see him again.

The car rolled to a stop. "We arrive, Mademoiselle. Give Madame Mercier my regards, please."

"What? Oh, yes. Thank you so much, Madame Lechard. I'll be back at the Ange Noir in a couple of days. Good-bye.

"Oh, and please, don't tell anyone where I am, no matter how important they say it is, unless. . . ."

"Yes, Mademoiselle Hanna? Unless?"

"Never mind. Just don't tell anyone at all. I'll be back soon."

Hanna banged the stag's head as Madame Lechard pulled away. The door opened, a deep, mellifluous voice said, "Mademoiselle Anders?"

"Yes."

"Madame Mercier is expecting you. Please come in."

In the half light of the vaulted entrance, Hanna saw a broad, powerful man, somewhat shorter than herself. He had a fair-skinned face under coarse white hair. Heavy silver eyebrows almost hid his deep-set eyes. He reminded Hanna of General Hal Martinson, a career Air Force man who had been her father's best friend.

"May I take your coat?"

"Thank you, no. I'll keep it with me."

He smiled. "I see you have been here before. Leave your traveling bag, I will take it to your room."

"Thank you."

"Madame Mercier is in the library. Come with me, please."

As the man led Hanna down the hallway she noticed he wore beautifully cut evening clothes. He had the square-shouldered carriage of a military man, but walked with an almost imperceptible limp. She was undecided. Was he servant, friend, or relative of Madame Mercier's?

He stopped in front of double doors and pulled them open, then stood back for Hanna to precede him.

She walked into a room that radiated a cozy welcome unusual for such a large space. There was a fireplace at one end, replete with mantel, columns, and pilasters in warm cherry wood. Red-shaded lamps shone on a carved library table. Except for a bank of windows on the outside wall, the room was filled with books from floor to ceiling. Three ladders on rolling tracks were available for access to the highest shelves.

Madame Mercier sat in a leather chair beside the fire. She looked up from her book and smiled.

"Mademoiselle Anders. I am pleased you consented to come. Please join me." She indicated a chair.

"I apologize for inviting you on such short notice. I see you did not have time to change for dinner."

"I painted in the Munster all day. Your note was at the desk when I arrived this evening. For personal reasons it was more convenient that I come right away."

"Of course. I am pleased that you did. I hope you have not dined, Clothilde has made something special. She enjoys cooking for guests."

"She won't find anyone more appreciative than I. Will there be time for me to bathe and dress?"

"Certainly. Jules will take you to your room, but first you must relax a moment. Have an aperitif with me." She poured viscous dark liquid from a Waterford decanter.

"Jules." She spoke to the man with the silver-thatched head, still waiting quietly by the door. "Please tell Clothilde she may serve in an hour, then return and show Mademoiselle Anders to her room."

"Oui, Madame."

"He works for you?" Hanna asked. "He doesn't seem like a servant."

"Jules is the husband of Clothilde, my cook. She grew up here at Tante Sophia's, her mother was a teacher, in Papa's time. Clothilde was never interested in studies, but she makes food the angels could enjoy.

"She married Jules after the war. He is French, and was a Resistance fighter with my husband. Wonderful people. And you are correct, they are more friends than employees."

"Do you miss having the school, Madame Mercier? Have you ever thought of reviving it?"

Madame smiled. "You are a perceptive young woman. I do

feel lonesome for *les jeunes filles* at times. If I were fifteen years younger, I might do it. Now. . . ." She shrugged.

"When Madame Lechard told me the place was closed, I felt lucky to have found you. A school named 'Tante Sophia's' and the family name Bonnard were all the clues I had."

"As long as I am alive the school will have a telephone listing. It is for the girls. They call from all over the world. Some are young women, some older than I. We are a clearinghouse for the locating of classmates."

"I hadn't thought of that. Do you ever have reunions?"

"Each year, on Founder's Day, August fourteenth. It is quite a celebration."

"Are your former students sad about the school being closed?"

"Oh, yes. We have fourth, fifth, sixth generation girls. I tell them there is hope, I have a niece who is intelligent, well educated. Perhaps when she is a little older. . . ."

"That would be nice." Hanna couldn't think of anything else to say.

Madame Mercier gave her a shrewd look. "You must wonder why I invited you to come. With your permission I will explain over dinner, when we can talk uninterrupted."

Jules returned and took Hanna upstairs and through a frigid, twisting corridor that ended in what looked like a temporary partition. He opened a door on the right, just before they reached the barrier. As they walked into the room he explained:

"All the area behind that partition was devoted to the school. Each floor is now blocked off in the same manner. Only the family living spaces are kept open."

"That seems sensible."

The bed was already turned down, a fire burned. Jules poked it up and added a log. He opened a door near the bed, revealing a bath.

Hanna saw a gigantic mahogany tub topped by tiers of brass pipes holding fluffy white towels. She couldn't wait to try it.

"May I be of further assistance?"

"No, thanks. This is lovely, I'll be fine."

After a last inspection of the room, he left. Hanna's bag was beside the bed. She opened it and unfolded a knit dress, then ran hot water into the tub.

Thirty minutes later she was bathed and dressed, looking into a full mirror that stood on a tilting cherry-wood frame. Her hair, still damp, fell in iridescent waves. She clasped a heavy gold chain around her neck and slipped on the sapphire ring. Now she could face Madame Mercier on something approaching an equal footing.

• • •

"Hanna. That is a pretty name," Madame Mercier commented as they were finishing dinner. Hanna had become impatient with the formal "Mademoiselle Anders" and asked to be called by her given name.

Madame pushed her dessert plate aside and pronounced, "My name is Helene. You must address me so."

Hanna nodded. "Talk of names reminds me. Since Dedushka first told me about the school, I've wondered why it was called Tante Sophia's."

Helene brushed a stray curl away from her temple and smiled. "Ah, that is a story in itself. Would you like to hear it?"

"Certainly."

"The school was founded in 1827, by a woman who called herself Cecile Bonnard. She inherited this house from a distant relative who had died impoverished. The place was in terrible disrepair.

"She came from London with her young son, telling the people of Basel she was a widow. She was quite lovely and stylish, and educated far beyond normal for the time. She dropped names right and left, 'Lord this, Lady that, Princess such and such.'

"She began to renovate the house immediately, and announced her intention to open a school for young ladies. Only those of the highest rank need apply.

"For some whimsical reason, she insisted money for the renovation and her other lavish expenditures came from a 'Tante Sophia,' who had died and left her a fortune. Hence the name of the school.

"We Bonnards are her descendants, but she is a complete mystery to us. We have not been able to trace her history beyond the time she arrived in Basel.

"Of course, at that time she created quite a stir, especially when word got around that there had been no beautiful young widow named Cecile Bonnard who moved in high circles of English society. Those whom she spoke of as intimates had never heard of her, at least not by that name.

"By then the school was well established. Mothers fought to get their daughters accepted. If anything, the hint of mystery gave her more prestige; perhaps she was a king's mistress, maybe her son was a royal bastard." Helene shrugged. "That is how people are."

"What a wonderful tale. I would have liked Cecile, I think.

"While we're on the subject of names, I'm curious about something else. What was Madeleine called when she lived here?"

"Madeleine Bonnard. I believe Ilse told people she was an orphaned relative."

"Dedushka told me 'Anders' came from the man who took him in after he was sent from Russia. Mr. Anders had been a merchant in Petrograd, he knew Dedushka's parents. Madeleine apparently added the 'on' to make Anderson."

"Such common sounding names for nobility. Your great-grandfather was the Grand Duke Peter Nicholaevich."

"Grand Duke Peter Nicholaevich. How elegant. And sort of phony, like a title made up for a character in an operetta."

Madame Mercier smiled. "I understand what you mean, but it is a little sad that you feel that way."

Hanna was thinking about the boy her grandfather had been and his small sister, two pampered children set adrift in the world. Dedushka was the older, he must have cried himself to sleep many a night, yearning for home, his mother and father.

How had the news come to him that his parents were dead, that he and his sister were all that was left of the family? What had he gone through to find Madeleine?

She pictured how eager he must have been for a reunion, how he must have dreamed of bringing her to the States, making a home for her. Then he had come to Switzerland and found that Madeleine considered Basel her home, the Bonnards her family.

"You are quiet, Hanna. You have had a tiring day?"

"Not really, I was just thinking of Dedushka and Madeleine, and how sad it was that they became estranged. I guess he made a mistake, insisting she go to America with him. But only the two of them were left. He must have felt responsible for her."

"I am sure that is true."

"Strange how people can cause so much grief, when they believe they're doing the right thing."

"Ah, you are a philosopher. We can only do our best, and hope things turn out well. As I did, in asking you here for a visit."

Here it comes, at last.

"When you telephoned Sunday, you were a voice speaking of the distant past. I had not thought of Madeleine since I received a letter from her, after I sent a cablegram informing her of Tante Ilse's death.

"The letter was eight pages long, rambling, almost incoherent. It was about her life here, and how happy she had been. I must confess I suspected her of being intoxicated when she wrote.

"She did not mention the box. I had completely forgotten it myself. When you spoke of it you seemed quite tense, as if it were important. I had supposed it contained pictures, letters, family mementoes. Nothing to be excited about.

"But after I saw your ring, suddenly I had the idea it might be filled with jewels, or other articles of value. So I thought I might open it myself, before I decided what to do about you."

"And did you?"

Helene Mercier shook her head. "Oh, no. I changed my mind. It would not have been honorable. Besides, the box is not here, it is at our chalet. I say 'our' because it has belonged to the family for several generations.

"Tante Ilse took it up there, a few years after Madeleine left, and stored it away in the back of a cabinet.

"That might seem silly to you, as large as this place is. But removing the box was a symbolic act, a repudiation, after she realized Madeleine would never return to Switzerland.

"You must understand, Ilse felt like a deserted parent. She wanted to strike back at someone who had hurt her. By then she rarely went to the chalet, so it seemed a good place to relegate the last tangible trace of Madeleine."

Hanna nodded. "Of course, she must have felt like Madeleine's mother. After all, Madeleine was a very young child when Ilse brought her from Russia. And she never came back after she went to America, even for a visit. I wonder why? Did she write often, at first?"

"As I recall letters came through with some frequency during the war. Tante Ilse always read them to the family at dinner. But then they came less often. When Ilse died, there had been no word for many years."

Hanna was fitting pieces of the puzzle together. "I told you I never met Madeleine, but Sunday I talked by telephone with a neighbor who had known her a long time. She said Madeleine was mentally unstable, with only brief spells of lucid behavior. The condition had existed a long time, she got worse every year."

Helene's long, supple hands with their white-tipped pink nails flew out in an expressive gesture.

"That could be the explanation! But how ironic. Tante Ilse died just a few years ago, her mind was sharp to the end. Perhaps the child she loved had become old and senile, long before she, herself, died."

Pretty Cici bounced into the room with fresh coffee; when she was gone Helene returned to the subject.

"About the box. Hanna, whatever it contains is yours. I am satisfied you are Madeleine's great-niece. If you agree, we will drive to the chalet tomorrow morning. We can discover the contents together."

"Oh, yes, please."

Helene stifled a small yawn. "It grows late. We shall want to be fresh for our trip. Shall we go up to bed?"

In Hanna's room, fresh logs crackled in the fireplace. The turned-down bed invited, she began to undress.

Only a few more hours and she would hold Dedushka's legacy in her own two hands. How could she be expected to sleep at a time like this?

She yawned.

S·I·X·T·E·E·N

HER body devoured sleep, gobbled it up with the voraciousness of a system starved for replenishment. Only the delicate brain sensors that monitored activity in the outside world were alert. They began to prod.

Wake up. Something weird's happening out there.

Let me alone.

Listen, you've gotta see about this.

It's a mouse. Somebody going to the bathroom.

No. Think I'd bother you with that kind of stuff? I'm not an alarmist. This is a biggie, I tell you.

There was a muffled crash, someone swore. Another voice hissed, "Silence, you ass!" followed by thumps and a rattle.

Hanna sat up in bed.

"Turn on the flash, there's a stinkin' damn partition across the hallway."

She struggled to shake off sleep and make sense of what she had heard. Or was this a nightmare?

A sharp crack followed a long, loud creak. Oh, God. The partition.

"If we do break it down, how in hell are we gonna find the redheaded bitch?"

That did it. Hanna jumped out of bed and ran out the door.

"Who is that?" she shouted. "Come through that wall and I'll blow your heads off!" she skittered through the dark passage and down the stairs to the first floor, yelling for Jules.

The house was vicious with cold, huge spaces of shadowed darkness loomed around her. At the foot of the stairs a bronze Diana stood in victorious splendor on the newel post, a dim electric torch extended from her up-flung left hand.

Hanna moved out of its range and leaned against the wall, gasping. She'd given up calling for Jules.

Coming downstairs might have been a mistake. Maybe Clothilde and Jules lived on the third floor; in TV shows servants lived under the eaves. Maybe she was trapped.

She could hide.

What about Helene? The two of them might be alone, maybe none of the staff lived in. The men were after Hanna, judging by what they said, but if they found Helene first . . .

Anything would be better than standing still. With a hand braced against the wall, she walked toward the back of the house. The passage ended in swinging doors. She pushed through into a kitchen lit by a dim night light.

"Jules!" she wailed.

Minutes passed.

"Qu'est-ce? . . . Mademoiselle Anders? What is wrong?"

A bright light appeared across the room, Hanna squinted against the glare. Jules and a short plump woman with gray braids came into the kitchen. The woman found a lamp beside the stove and lit it.

A black dressing gown hung from Jules' shoulders, his hair stood up in tails. Even so, his innate dignity saved him from looking ridiculous. He reached for the belt and tied it, then ran fingers through his hair.

"Are you ill, Mademoiselle? Has something frightened you?"

"Someone's broken into the house. They're at the partition in the second-floor hall, right by my bedroom. I heard them talking."

Jules didn't argue or ask questions. He said something to his wife, disappeared, and came back holding a gun.

"Stay with Clothilde, Mademoiselle. I will see about your intruders."

"Be careful!"

He was already gone.

"Do not worry, Mademoiselle. Jules takes care of himself. It would be better to pity the bandits.

"But look at you! Your feet are bare, and your arms. . . ." Clothilde broke off with a clucking noise.

Hanna realized she was shaking like an aspen in a blizzard. Her feet were purple, chill bumps covered her arms.

Still clucking, Clothilde disappeared into her quarters and returned with slippers and a chenille robe.

Hanna put them on and sat on a slat-backed chair at the kitchen table. The cook lit a burner on the black monster of a stove that loomed in a corner, and made coffee. They drank one cup. Another.

Hanna's ears strained for sounds. The old house was quiet, but it was a stealthy kind of silence. As though it could be sheltering any number of nasty presences.

Jules didn't come back. Clothilde seemed unperturbed, but a knot of anxiety developed in Hanna's stomach.

It was almost an anticlimax when he finally came in and sat at the table. He began to talk, appearing to choose his words with care.

"There is no one upstairs now, Mademoiselle. The only usable door into the school side is on this floor. Prowlers could not find it easily; and anyway, it is secure.

"I will search the other side of the building in the morning. Now I believe we should all get some sleep."

He gave Hanna a look of sympathetic concern. "This is an old pile of stone, Mademoiselle, with many noises. One grows used to them, but for a stranger . . . is it possible you were dreaming?"

"No! The voices spoke English . . ." Her sentence trailed off. Of course they would speak English, if they had come from her own subconscious.

"You are frightened, Mademoiselle, in a strange house, a foreign country. I will bring a bedroll and sleep outside your room until morning."

"Oh, no, I couldn't let you, Jules." A form protest only. Hanna knew she wouldn't be able to go back to that room and stay alone.

Jules understood. "It is settled. We will go upstairs now, Clothilde will bring what is necessary for me."

• • •

Frank Rivera felt a sneeze coming on. He made a halfhearted attempt to stifle it. No joy.

"Aaa-chooo. Damn it! Sonofabitch!" The words were a savage comment to thorns that had raked his cheek when he sneezed.

He was crouched against a brick garden wall across the street from number 23, Stillestrasse, concealed by a tangle of climbing rose runners that were quick to punish his slightest move.

It had been an interesting night. As far as he knew Hanna Anders was still inside, but he wasn't sure about the state of her health. LeBeau, Hippolyte the Hulk, and some other scumbag had boosted their way through a window on the other side of the building at three A.M. Frank had been on a recon tour, and had barely seen them in time to take cover.

The operation looked like something out of a third-rate movie. The window was shattered with a quick blow, two muscular giants vaulted inside easily. Jackie LeBeau jumped, missed the sill, and fell back. He tried again. Fell again.

Frank watched with glee as Hippo dropped to the ground and lifted LeBeau into the waiting arms of sleaze number two.

It didn't take Frank long to stop laughing. Only thing funny about LeBeau was the giant ego inside that pint-sized body. Malevolent little bastard.

He thought about going to the nearest phone kiosk to confer with Clete, but he was afraid to leave.

Time dragged, leaden minute after minute. When they hadn't come back by 3:45, Frank couldn't take the inactivity any longer. He eased his way to the front of the house.

Inspecting the building with a trained eye, he saw a faint oblong of light on the second floor that hadn't been there before. Nothing else.

He hot-footed it around to the broken window, in time to see three shadows disappear up the alley. A few minutes later a car, lights extinguished, rolled past. He waited a good while before returning to his command post inside the rose vines.

That had been three hours before. He rubbed an itch on his nose and thought about things in general. Instinct told him LeBeau's Raiders had turned up a big goose egg. How could they have found her in a place like that, in forty-five minutes? Let alone forced her to give up the triptych?

Frank needed a smoke. He reached for the pack, and froze mid-gesture as he heard the distinctive crunch of tires on cobblestone. A dark shape rolled past. The Mercedes had returned.

Hot damn, I was right. Didn't get a thing but glass splinters in your butts, did you, boys?

He slumped against the wall, the cigarette forgotten. He was ready to get back to the pension and catch some sleep. Clete would come to relieve him at nine. With any kind of luck, everything would be peaceful until then.

S·E·V·E·N·T·E·E·N

WHAT do you eat for your morning meal in Denver, Colorado, Hanna?"

Hanna was tempted to answer "coyote steak, fillet of grizzly, and prairie chicken eggs."

She played it straight. "A bowl of granola or a carton of yogurt on weekdays. Sometimes on Sunday I have friends over and fix a country breakfast: scrambled eggs, ham, biscuits, and red-eye gravy."

Helene didn't bite on the red-eye gravy lure.

They sat at a small table in a room just off the kitchen, watching Cici serve coffee, crusty home-baked bread, and fresh fruit from heaven knew where. The room had once been a pantry and storage area, Helene told her. High-ceilinged, with plaster walls, it was decorated in butter yellow and blue, with solid old French furniture.

Hanna was impatient with police chit-chat, she wanted to ask if her hostess knew about the prowlers.

Helene put down her fork and leaned forward. "Jules tells me you had a bad experience last night."

Ha, I'm learning the rules. Be patient and she'll get around to the subject you want to talk about. Rush her and you get stonewalled.

"I know he thinks I was imagining things, but. . . ."

"But he does not, at least not this morning. There is a window broken on the school side. I suspect neighborhood boys, who know that portion of the house is not lived in. Nothing was taken, and no damage done other than the window."

"Helene, they spoke English. Someone mentioned my name. At least I think he did. Anyway, he said the redheaded . . . never mind what he called me. But it was American slang."

Helene clapped her palms. "I have the explanation! I should have thought of it sooner. Cici! The little witch, he was looking for her. Did I tell you she has an American boyfriend? How naughty of him, I really must speak to her about it."

"But . . ." How could Hanna make this woman admit the break-in was more than a prank?

"Helene, I haven't mentioned this before, but the second day I was in Basel I was molested in the street by a man. I don't know what he would have done if it hadn't been for . . . that's another story. Other things have happened since then. I believe someone—"

"How unfortunate! What a terrible thing, and just after you arrived," Helene cut in. "You must have a very bad impression of this city. You are a lovely girl, still, you must not believe all Swiss men are so impetuous. That kind of thing is extremely rare, I assure you.

"Now. We must talk about our trip. As you know, I instructed Cici to awaken you at seven, so we could make an early start. We will motor through a village called Langenbruck. It is charming, I thought you might enjoy spending a few hours there. We will lunch at the inn, then go on to the chalet, arriving midafternoon.

"Oh, and take a small suitcase with you, in the event we decide to stay overnight. Does that sound agreeable?"

"Of course, it sounds lovely." Hanna gave up. Helene was not going to take the night's invasion seriously, much less believe it had any connection with Hanna. Like a good hostess she was diverting conversation to a more pleasant subject.

"Excellent." Helene stood and brushed crumbs from her skirt. "It is now eight o'clock. Can you be ready in fifteen minutes?"

"Yes, of course."

"Then we will meet in the kitchen at fifteen past eight. We go to the automobile from there. Be sure to wear something warm, it will be very cold in the chalet until we get fires going."

• • •

Hanna walked into the kitchen a few minutes early. Helene was already there, giving instructions to Cici and Clothilde. Hanna noticed her voice sounded like a young woman's, warm and vital, spiced with pleasurable excitement.

Helene saw her come in and switched from French to English. "*Cherie,* you are very prompt." She picked up a monogrammed leather case and waved a beckoning hand. "We go."

Hanna said a quick good-bye to Cici, then asked Clothilde about Jules.

"He is lazy this morning, Mademoiselle. He has returned to his bed to sleep awhile longer."

"Please thank him for his patience last night. And thank you for the robe and slippers, I left them in my room."

She hurried after Helene into the brick courtyard. A yellow BMW was parked in front of a stable that had been partially converted into garages. Helene unlocked the trunk and they stowed their luggage.

On the surface it was a cheerful morning, crisp and clear. A few stars were still visible, sunrise was delayed by a band of black cloud over the eastern horizon. There seemed to be a restless cruelty in the early chill, promising something nasty for the day.

The courtyard and stable were closed in by the house on two sides, the other two were bounded by an eight-foot stone wall. At the south of the compound were heavy iron gates, opening onto Stillestrasse.

Helene pulled up to the gates and stopped. She opened the car door, Hanna asked, "May I help?"

"Thank you, *cherie,* there is no need. The gates are well balanced, they move easily."

Hanna touched her arm. "Helene, wait."

"Oui?"

"This will sound silly. Please consider it an attack of nerves, and humor me. When you drive through the gate I'm going to lean over in the seat. If anyone happens to be watching they'll think you're alone."

Helene's laugh trilled. "*Mais oui*, if it pleases you. We will have an adventure, like on American television." She got out and opened the gates, humming the familiar dum-da-dum-dum theme from *Dragnet*.

Hanna hunched over, her long hair spilling onto the floorboards.

• • •

Something was damned well coming down, Frank could feel it. He cursed Octavian, Jackie LeBeau, women, Switzerland, winter, and Clete Cross, with fine impartiality. He squinted at his watch. Five after eight, less than an hour and he could turn the whole damn Stillestrasse circus over to Clete.

It wouldn't fall out that way. Hell no, of course it wouldn't.

Morning still hovered on the brink of daylight. Frank's eyes burned. Eye drops would help, but they were in the Peugeot, parked two blocks away. On a busier street, where it wouldn't be likely to attract attention.

His feeling of impending action persisted. He decided to go after the goddamn car.

He stayed in the shadows, walking as fast as he dared. His rubber-soled shoes made a scrunching noise when he hit a patch of gravel, he mouthed a silent curse.

The Mercedes hadn't shown up again, but he knew it was in the vicinity. Parked, while LeBeau and Company spied on that silent stone hulk, same as he was doing. He'd just as soon avoid their attention. He wasn't pissed off enough to take on all three of them. Not yet.

He eased inside the Peugeot, found the small plastic bottle, and put a drop of liquid in each eye. Damn, that burned. He had a swig of coffee and drove back to Stillestrasse. Leaving the car on a side street with its nose ten feet from the intersection, he got out to look around.

Sculptured gargoyles and rain-spouts on the gray mansion at number 23 were beginning to stand out in the increasing light. He watched with predatory concentration. As if he had willed it to happen, iron gates swung open a hundred yards south of the front entrance.

"Hot damn, here we go."

A light-colored BMW pulled into the street and stopped, the driver got out and shut the gates. A woman, not tall enough to be Hanna. The car pulled away, powerful engine throbbing as it accelerated.

It looked like the woman was alone. Frank didn't buy it. He ran for the Peugeot, gunned his own engine to life, clutched, and eased the shift into first gear.

And thought how Clete would be more pissed at missing the action than he was about getting caught up in it.

Clete was high-strung, one of those eager beavers who always had his hand up to volunteer before he knew damn-all about what he was getting into. Never enough sense to back off, had to be right in the thick of everything.

Frank and Clete were born to be natural enemies, like the mongoose and the snake. Boston-raised Harvard grad and street-wise Bronx. Hell of it was, they'd liked each other from the first. No goddamn way to figure it.

Not that Clete was a snot-nose. He sure as hell wasn't

squeamish or lily-livered. If he ever had been, 'Nam had fixed that.

• • •

A small man in elegant, filthy trousers and a ripped vicuna overcoat huddled shivering on the corner south of number 23. He watched the BMW leave. After that a silent Peugeot without lights rounded the corner to follow, like a homing missile.

Jackie LeBeau had seen a woman in the BMW, but she damn sure wasn't Hanna Anders. If that was Cross following he'd bitten on a kindergarten scam, his girlfriend was still inside.

Jackie indulged himself, thinking what he'd do to the red-headed bitch when he got his hands on her. He imagined her eyes popping with fear; her face ugly, drained of blood. He'd make her apologize. Make her beg. "Please, Jackie, don't hurt me. Don't kill me." Kneeling, so she could look up at him.

She'd been so bitchin' clever last night. Made him believe she had to go to the head, left him cooling his heels with two plates of bloody veal something-or-other congealing in grease, and a hovering waiter who sniggered and pretended not to notice.

Jackie LeBeau had fallen for a trick old as the hills. Fifteen minutes he'd sat like a dumb-ass jerk, wondering what the hell was wrong. Bitch.

He popped a Darvon, chased it with two Gelusil.

If that retardate Hippolyte hadn't gotten lucky and seen her slip out a private entrance and take off with some old broad, she'd have gotten by with it. Been gone, slick as hell. Jackie's roasted ass would have been served on a platter, Octavian carving.

His stomach rumbled, he spat. He'd made her sorry, the bloody bitch. Maybe he'd let her live. Just carve her up a little, give her something to remember Jackie LeBeau.

Had to keep his head from now on, the break-in was pure folly. Hippolyte's idea, but his own fault. He was in charge. He would have vetoed it, except by then he was so crazy to get his hands on her he'd have agreed to call in the Mongolian army if someone suggested it.

They must have looked like the bloody Three Stooges, stumbling around in that stone heap. Damn miracle they hadn't had their heads blown off.

He stamped numb feet, needles of pain shot up through his ankles. A time check told him it was a few minutes past eight-thirty. He didn't figure anyone else would leave number 23 for a while, better go back and use the car phone to make a report to Octavian.

That brought up another problem. Could he trust Hippolyte and Dieter not to mention the break-in?

Yeah. They hadn't exactly covered themselves in glory. Besides, even they were smart enough not to make an enemy of Jackie LeBeau.

He was nervous about Octavian, they hadn't parted on the best of terms. Octavian made it clear his faith in Jackie was shaken, Jackie falling for such an old scam. Woman going to "powder her nose." Another score to settle with Hanna Anders.

He couldn't get his mind off it. The sick realization she wasn't coming back. A last hope she'd gotten some kind of female complaint and gone to her room. A telephone call had settled that.

He'd looked outside, though, and her car was still there. After that he jabbed the elevator button and rode up at a goddamn snail's pace, then unleashed his anger on the door to her room; yelling, hammering the solid wood until heads popped out all along the hallway. People glared. One skinny ass in undershorts yelled an insult and gave him the finger. Jackie'd have punched him out, but there wasn't time.

He couldn't find Hippo or Dieter. They must've sneaked into a bar for a fast belt. So then he'd had to take a cab back to face Octavian, apprehension gnawing a hole in his gut.

He still didn't want to think about what might have happened if the phone hadn't rung as he started to explain how he let the bitch get away from him.

It was Hippo, full of himself for catching the broad when she dodged out. He and Dieter had followed her. When the old dame let Anders out and drove off, Dieter staked out the house and Hippo hot-footed it to a phone.

So it had been another cab for Jackie, Octavian's furious rhetoric ringing in his ears as he rode to number 23, Stillestrasse.

Now he looked balefully at the house. Soon as he saw this place the night before, he'd known what it must be. Ilse Bonnard's school, where the Anderson broad had lived when she was a kid. They'd gotten that much out if the crazy old bat before they offed her.

Bonnard must be dead. Who lived there now? How many of them? Damned triptych wasn't even there, he'd bet on it. Thing could be anywhere, after all these years. It would be a bloody damn miracle to rival the second coming if somebody hadn't sold that baby by now.

Octavian said not. His theory was, it was impossible for a work of art that rare to hit the market without a lot of publicity.

Jackie figured it could have been sold privately to some mega-millionaire who'd front a bundle and no questions asked. Like Octavian himself. There were others of his kind. Dime a dozen in the Arab countries.

He reached the Mercedes, parked behind a truck that had one wheel missing. Jackie slid in and snarled at Dieter to stop snoring while he was on the phone.

Twenty minutes later he crashed the stag's head knocker against its metal rest. Only his eyes were alive, they glittered in a face frozen with fury. Octavian had never talked to him like that before, like he had the brains of a shithouse mouse. He was scared. He wanted to hurt somebody.

He pulled the Uzi from its underarm sling, Dieter and Hippolyte followed suit.

The massive door opened. A girl in a smart gray uniform

chirped an inquiry as she hastily finger-combed spiky black hair. Hippo knocked her down. She began to scream. They shoved inside and slammed the door.

"Shut up." Jackie squatted and rammed his Uzi against her throat. She choked the scream to a gurgle, her eyes dilated.

Jackie smiled.

E·I·G·H·T·E·E·N

THE BMW hit a patch of ice and skidded to the left. Hanna woke, clutched reflexively at the armrest, and looked out her window. Outcroppings of rock and snowy clumps of pine and spruce crowded the narrow road. To the driver's side there was nothing but roiling, flat-bottomed clouds driven by what would have been called a Norther at home.

She wasn't nervous. Mountain bred herself, she recognized Helene as a skillful driver. She leaned back and closed her eyes, reluctant to break the companionable silence.

It hadn't been long since they'd left the resort village of Langenbruck, on the Upper Hauenstein Pass. With Helene playing tour guide, they had roamed the picturesque streets, Hanna half expecting to see a chorus of men in feathered hats and liederhosen appear.

Finally the wind forced them to seek shelter. They lunched at the inn, as Helene had promised, before starting the steep climb to the chalet. Lulled by exercise, food, and the rhythmic noise of the engine, Hanna had fallen asleep.

All day she'd refused to think of anything but the moment, the trip, and her anticipation of opening the Russian box. Now, relaxed and unwary, she thought of Clete.

How could he have made such a potent impression? She had seen him, what? Four, five times? She ticked them off. At the train station; on the street after he came to her rescue; at dinner the next night; in the Cathedral; and back at the Ange Noir. Just before she ran out on him.

It's true, I won't ever see him again. How would he find me? Unless he hangs around until I get back.

In a pig's eye, he will. Clete Cross isn't the type to moon around after a woman.

Of course if he's involved in the weird stuff that's been happening he might turn up. Then I wouldn't want to see him.

What if I hadn't run away? If I could just be with him one more time. In the lobby he promised to tell me all about himself, whatever I wanted to know. There could be an explanation. . . .

Sure. He's your guardian angel. Believe it.

It's possible he's not a crook, damn it. I'll never know unless he has a chance to explain.

"Hanna? Are you awake?"

She sat up and yawned. "I am now. Sorry I faded away like that. I ate too much back at the inn. And it's so restful looking out the window at the mountains, with snowflakes beginning to fall. Besides, I always go to sleep in the car. When I'm not driving, of course."

Helene laughed. "I certainly hope not while you are driving yourself.

"You did not sleep well last night. It is good for you to catch up a little."

"Are we far from the chalet?"

"Only a short distance in kilometers, but we go slowly because of the road, the snow. Twenty minutes, perhaps."

"Helene, tell me more about my great-grandparents. Did Ilse talk about them much? Or Madeleine?"

Helene shook her head. "Not Madeleine. I never heard her mention her home in Russia, or her parents. I'm not sure she remembered anything about them.

"Tante Ilse . . . that was a different matter. It will do no harm to speak of it now, to tell her secret.

"She was in love with Petra, your great-grandfather. The husband of her dearest friend, Lisanne.

"Oh, do not think there was anything improper between them. Here is how Ilse explained it when she was very old, and wanted to tell about the past.

"Ilse and Lisanne talked my grandparents into giving them a trip to the French Riviera, when they were seventeen years old and had completed their studies. Lisanne's father had gambled away all his money by then, she rarely heard from him. Ilse loved her like a sister. My grandparents had almost adopted her, they gladly paid for both girls to go.

"They stayed with schoolmates, moving from one place to another as fancy took them. I'm not sure where they first met Petra, or rather Ilse met him. She had attended a dance, Lisanne stayed home with a sore throat.

"Petra was at the party, in fact he was the guest of honor. Ilse thought he was quite the handsomest thing she had ever seen, and couldn't rest until she had managed an introduction.

"From what I have been told, Ilse was very witty as a girl. Petra liked her. A friendship developed."

Helene broke off, her attention diverted by a narrow hairpin turn. When the dangerous spot was behind them Hanna urged, "Please go on."

"Before I tell more I will describe the two girls. From Ilse's recollections, and then there are photographs taken during their school days."

"You have the pictures? I'd love to see them."

Helene nodded acquiescence. "Ilse was tall and thin, she had strong features, lovely hair, and carried herself with pride.

"Lisanne was quite simply stunning, there is no other way to describe her. Short, with curly dark hair, huge eyes that Ilse called smoky gray, with long lashes; and the kind of figure that was much prized in those days. Full in the bosom, tiny waist, rounded hips."

"I recognize the type," Hanna muttered.

Helene glanced at her. "From the pictures, her face was not unlike yours, although your coloring is certainly different."

Laughter bubbled up in Hanna. The thought of a resemblance between herself and an Edwardian pocket Venus was too much.

Helene saw the humor. "Your build is different, I will admit."

"Go on, please. What happened? Did Petra abandon Ilse for the seductive Lisanne?"

"Something like that. Petra called on Ilse a few times in the home where the girls were guests. She told me those were the most wonderful days of her life, although common sense told her a man of his nobility and wealth would never become seriously involved with the daughter of a Swiss schoolmaster, no matter how prosperous or exclusive the school.

"It was a while before he saw Lisanne. After she recovered from her sore throat, she resumed her busy social schedule. Eligible bachelors constantly invited her out.

"She did find time to tease Ilse about her mysterious beau, and demand to meet him, but Ilse was in no hurry for that to happen.

"Then one night Petra called for Ilse at a time when Lisanne was in the parlor waiting for friends to come by. According to Ilse, one look and it was all over."

"Didn't Lisanne have any qualms about stealing her best friend's man?"

Helene shrugged. "Ilse did not blame her, heartbroken though she was. Petra bombarded Lisanne with flowers, notes, gifts. What made it even worse was that he made Ilse his confidante, about how much he adored Lisanne. He considered Ilse a good friend, no more. What is your American slang word? A 'pal'? Almost as if she were another man."

"So Lisanne was swept away by Petra's attention, and Ilse was a good sport about it. I may be descended from Lisanne, but I identify with Ilse."

"You are a kind young woman, Hanna.

"To go on with the story, Petra ignored his family's protests about a marriage. After all, Lisanne was from an aristocratic family even if there was no longer any money. Petra was rich enough for both of them. So there was a big wedding, and Ilse was Lisanne's maid of honor. It was quite a social affair."

"No doubt."

"And a great honor to Ilse, to be a member of the wedding party. A schoolmaster's daughter among royalty.

"Ilse said she was not altogether unselfish in giving the match her blessing. Lisanne and Petra were the two people she loved most in the world, that way she could still be with them.

"She visited Russia for two months every year, when she could get away from the school. Ilse was teaching by then."

"Was it on one of those visits that she smuggled Madeleine out of Russia?"

"Yes. In the summer of 1916 Ilse's parents wished her to remain in Switzerland. Russia was in turmoil; fighting a war against Kaiser Wilhelm. Also, there were already rumors of internal strife. They felt she would be in danger.

"They were right, of course. But Ilse said Lisanne needed her, and insisted on going.

"When it came time for her to return, she sent a letter saying she would stay with Lisanne awhile longer, and perhaps bring the family to Basel for a visit. It was in the next few weeks that she escaped with the child."

"Do you know if Ilse ever heard from Lisanne or Petra again?"

Helene shook her head. "Not that I know of.

"Ilse would never speak of their deaths, until the last week of her life. As I think I told you, her mind was very sharp. She suddenly became obsessed with talking about Lisanne and Petra.

"She told me how much she resented them being killed. As though they had died to spite her, deprive her of their company.

" 'It is not fair,' she told me. 'I have grown old and ugly; they are always young, beautiful, passionate.'

"I did not know what to say. I never dreamed she could feel like that, she had always spoken of Lisanne with such love and respect. As though she were a dead saint."

Hanna was thoughtful, absorbing the story. Finally she said, "Lisanne met Petra on a trip that was paid for by Ilse's parents. She took him away from Ilse."

"That is true."

"Ilse never married. She raised Lisanne's daughter as if the child were her own. Then Madeleine left, and never visited her foster mother again."

Helene nodded.

"My family hasn't treated yours with much consideration. I wonder that you agreed to see me at all."

Helene's shoulders sketched one of her shrugs. "I believe none of it was intentional. Lisanne and Petra did not cause the Russian Revolution.

"As for Madeleine, I think now her mind must have always been . . . a bit disturbed. When you telephoned I did not feel any malice."

She chuckled. "But I was not particularly eager to make your acquaintance, either." She put a gloved hand on Hanna's arm.

"I am happy we have met. It is like a circle, a completion, is it not? I like you. And we are having our own little adventure."

"For me, a big adventure."

"But, *cherie,* we have only talked about the past, people dead and gone. Tell me about yourself. I want to know all about the place where you live."

Hanna described as best she could what it was like to live in Denver. Helene could relate to the physical description of the countryside well enough, as Hanna drew parallels to the Alps. But how to make someone with Helene's background understand the informality, the free and easy manner of the American West? She tried, and Helene listened politely.

"That is interesting, *cherie,* but you have not spoke about yourself. Are you in love, do you have a wonderful man waiting for you to come home?

Hanna was embarrassed, and that made her angry with herself. Her answer came in awkward spurts.

"Nothing like that. I mean, I have plenty of male friends. Nobody special. Not now.

"I fell in love a few times in college, and later when I was in art school. Like everyone does. Nothing came of it.

"Someone will come along, I suppose. I'm not ready for anything serious, I have to keep my mind on painting right now. Want to keep my mind on it. I love to paint, it's my life. Maybe I'll never have time for marriage."

"Ah, yes." Helene pointed up and to her right. "See that great rock formation hanging over the road? It resembles a stooped old woman, do you not think so? We are only a kilometer from the chalet."

The tactful change of subject was not lost on Hanna.

She knew I was uncomfortable talking about myself, and let me off the hook. That was considerate. She's more complex than comes across at first glance.

"Helene, after all this time, why didn't you ever look in the box? Weren't you curious?"

"I never thought about it. Someone else's family papers, photographs, keepsakes. I had forgotten it existed until you mentioned it. Now I am almost as eager as you, since you say your grandfather hinted it might contain something valuable."

"He did more than hint, Helene."

In the past few minutes the lazy snowflakes had ceased, now hard-driven clouds spat round, icy pellets that crumbled as they hit the windshield. Helene turned the wipers on and looked at Hanna.

"Are you worried about the weather? We are in no danger of being trapped at the chalet. I will tell you a little story about my husband, to explain.

"He was a pilot. He had been educated in England. When things looked bleak for the British at the beginning of World War II, he joined the Royal Air Force. He was shot down over France, and became a part of the French Resistance. That is when he met Jules.

"During the war he developed a love affair with anything that flew; it lasted all his life. When he was financially able, he bought one airplane. Then as he prospered, another, and another.

"He was not a young man when we married, and rarely piloted himself anymore. He employed a professional. We owned a small French business jet and a helicopter. We had a helicopter landing pad built beside the chalet for quick trips, and to fly guests in.

"When he died I sold both aircraft, but the pad is still maintained. There is a charter service in Basel, I have used it in the past."

"You leave your car up here?"

"Yes. When the roads are clear, Jules comes up after it. We have two others."

She talks of abandoning a new BMW to the mercies of an Alpine winter as if it were a kiddy car. It shouldn't surprise me, I guess. I seem to have a hard time adjusting to the caprices of the very wealthy.

A clearing opened on the right. Hanna saw a half-timbered stone building with an overhanging shingle roof. Between it and the road was a neat garden, bisected by a path. Snow covered everything.

On either side and behind the chalet rock spills and clumps of trees made a rough, beautiful landscape. Helene turned into a drive just beyond the garden and stopped on a round parking area. Behind it Hanna saw the helipad chiseled out of surrounding rock, with perimeter lights on poles. A red wind sock snapped sharply.

They got out of the car, retrieved their cases, and walked

toward the front door. Helene stopped to look at the chalet. Her face expressed pleasure.

"I haven't been here since early summer. This place is so beautiful to me, so tied with happy memories. I should come more often."

Hanna took in details with the acute observation of an artist. Pale gray stone walls, exposed Tyrolean woodwork that stood out in bold relief. There was an elaborate, carved balcony that ran the length of the second floor, on the side facing the parking area. The path they stood on led to an off-center door, with a series of multipaned casement windows on the left.

"Once we employed a caretaker who made his home here. Now it is difficult to find anyone who wants to live in such isolation. An old man down the road cares for the grounds, and supplies firewood in winter.

"When I come I always bring Jules and Clothilde, sometimes Cici if I am having guests. This time is different, though. I wanted the two of us to be alone, I thought we would become better acquainted that way."

She unlocked the door and led Hanna into a room that looked like a movie set Bavarian hunting lodge, with rustic wooden furniture upholstered in animal skins. Hanna thought the skins must have looked better on the animals.

Helene walked to the fireplace, knelt, struck a giant match on rough stone. When she rose a fire was blazing.

"How did you do that so quickly?"

"There a starting device of bottled gas that shuts off automatically after a few minutes. A former student brought it to me."

"Thoughtful gift." Hanna pulled a chair closer to the fire.

"Stay here and warm yourself, I will be right back." Helene disappeared through a door under the staircase.

Hanna huddled in the chair, pulling the collar of her coat close around her neck. She felt the warm fleece against her skin.

I'm a hypocrite. Critical of Helene's pelt upholstery, but I wear sheepskin.

She examined her surroundings. The staircase was directly in front of the outside door, against the south wall. They had left their luggage by the bottom step.

She thought about spending the night in the chalet, and shuddered to think how cold the bedrooms would be.

Helene came back carrying a beaker and two cups. She poured and gave a cup to Hanna. It smelled of spices, butter, and rum. Hanna tasted it.

"This is heaven. Thank you."

The fire blazed higher, the rum did its job. Hanna shrugged out of her coat.

"Keep that with you, the rest of the chalet is not warm yet."

Hanna thought of suggesting they light fires upstairs, so it would be comfortable when they went to bed.

No. Helene would think of her as another pampered American. Europeans didn't seem to mind icy bedchambers, they burrowed into thick envelopes of eiderdown like hibernating moles.

"There is fresh wood laid out on the bedroom hearths. I will light the fires later. It will be quite pleasant by bedtime."

There she goes, reading my mind again.

Hanna finished her drink. She was fired up to get on with the purpose of their visit. "You said Ilse brought Madeleine's box here and stored it in a kitchen cabinet?"

Way to go, Hanna. Subtle hint.

Helene savored the last of her rum. "Yes. I see you are anxious to solve the mystery of your family treasure. Come with me."

They walked into a small room filled with pegs for hanging outer-wear and household equipment, then on to a cold, dark dining room. Hanna was sorry she hadn't taken Helene's advice about bringing her coat.

They turned left through a swinging door into the kitchen, warmth and light greeted them. Hanna walked toward the source of heat, an open-hearth fireplace in the partition wall that shared a chimney with the sitting-room fireplace. On either side were cabinets, built into the wall and running the length of the room.

Beside the sink was a square window, the only one in the kitchen. The back wall contained a narrow outside door with heavy wooden bars across it, and a restaurant-size refrigerator and freezer. In the center of the room was a plank table with six chairs.

Hanna looked up at the branched light fixture, a curious thing made of deer antlers. "Where does your electricity come from?"

"We have our own generator. It works well enough if we are careful. One day I will have a more powerful one installed."

She walked to the upper cabinet closest to the hearth. Opening it, she reached in and groped blindly. Then, with a sigh of exasperation, she pulled a chair over and stood on it.

"May I help you?"

"Yes, just come and take things as I hand them to you. These cabinets are deep, and of course Ilse must have pushed Lisanne's box to the very back." She gave Hanna a thrill of apprehension by adding, "Surely no one would have moved it."

Hanna hurried to help, watching Helene's every move with the intent fascination of a chicken hawk eyeing a fat squab. As she reached out to take an armload of miscellaneous objects, her toe caught in a rag mat in front of the fireplace. She stumbled and caught herself against the inside fire wall. Her knee cracked against a hard protuberance; she bent to rub the injured spot with sooty fingers.

Helene was beside her, making sympathetic noises. "Are you hurt? *Tiens*, you are full of cinder. I will get you a damp sponge." She hurried to the sink, moving with the darting grace of a hummingbird.

Hanna was more embarrassed than hurt except for her left knee, which had found whatever it was she had banged it against. She bent to investigate. There was a ringed knob welded to an iron rectangle in the blackened stone.

Helene bustled back with the wet sponge and a towel. Hanna wiped her hands and asked, "What's that insert in the stone for? There, inside the fireplace?"

Helene looked. "Oh, that is a warming oven. Once food was cooked, it was put inside to stay hot until served. It hasn't been used since I can remember, I doubt if it would open, now.

"Are you hurt?" she asked again.

"Not a bit, just clumsy. I'm ready to help, if you can trust me not to break anything."

Helene climbed back on the chair. "Yes, of course. Take these, if you will." She handed down a pair of tarnished candlesticks. Hanna conveyed them to the table.

"And these." An armload of linen tablecloths and napkins spilled out.

"I can touch it." Helene was buried inside the cabinet, her voice muffled. A sprinkle of goose bumps executed a glissade between Hanna's shoulder blades.

Helene backed out of the cabinet, Hanna steadied her chair. She emerged with a carved wooden box, and passed it down with elaborate care before she climbed off the chair.

It was heavy. Hanna carried it to the table without breathing. She shoved aside the linen cloths and set it down, releasing the air pent up in her lungs in a long sigh.

The Russian inheritance. At last.

N·I·N·E·T·E·E·N

IN the pension where Clete Cross waited there was one telephone on the second floor, a solid, important black instrument that occupied an alcove at the head of the stairs. Clete glared at it. He walked back to his room, left the door open, and dropped into a chair.

His face was ugly with pain. The pupil of his left eye dilated, the eye itself felt in danger of bulging out of the socket. Vessels gorged with hot, turgid blood ruthlessly expanded against his brain. Light hurt, the movement of his eyeballs hurt. His head contained a nightmare beast who gnawed greedily, feeding on anxiety and tension.

A Chinese friend had shown him key spots in the temples and the base of the neck. If the right degree of pressure could be applied in just the right place, a vascular headache was magically relieved. Clete had used the technique with varying degrees of success.

He tried it now.

Frank bitched about ulcers. Clete envied him. Nothing in your gut could hurt like this.

The acupressure didn't work. He pawed through his shaving case for a bottle of Fiorinal. Precious, horded capsules, resorted to only in extremity. He found them, sipped water from the carafe beside his bed, and downed two.

Seemed like all he had done lately was sit around on his ass and wait for crumbs of information from Frank. It didn't help to remind himself that things worked like that sometimes. A two-man team splits watches, one of them gets all the action.

He laid his head back against the chair, waiting for the pain to subside. Inactivity gave him too much time to speculate about how he'd handled things.

Like last night. He *was* ready to level with Hanna, damn it. Tell her what he was after and demand to know what the hell she was up to. Get the cards on the table, go from there.

She ran out on him.

Because he scared her, or had that been the plan all along? Play innocent victim of circumstance until she could walk with the triptych?

Why in hell had he let her go upstairs by herself? He should have known better, stuck with her instead of that scumbag LeBeau.

It would have been risky, though, without Frank around to help. Frank had gone to stake out the house on Stillestrasse at six, like they planned.

Okay then, Clete should have insisted she go straight from the lobby, she could have bought a toothbrush and nightie somewhere.

She might have refused, made a scene. People everywhere, LeBeau in the dining room, Hippo and his clone had to be somewhere near. No, he couldn't have taken the chance.

The Fiorinal began to work, easing the iron maiden that clutched his skull. He walked to the window.

Nothing. A quiet street down there, anything unusual would stick out like a whore at a Baptist revival.

At least LeBeau had come out looking like more of a fool than he had. Clete grinned, remembering. LeBeau had shot out of the dining room and snapped questions at the girl on the desk. He could tell by LeBeau's attitude that she didn't tell him anything. LeBeau used the desk phone, ran to check Hanna's car, then made for the elevator.

Clete had abandoned cover and sprinted for the stairs, almost breaking his neck over a poodle leashed to a pillar. He ran up two flights top speed and was sucking air like a wind-broke horse when he got to Hanna's door.

"Come out, Hanna, LeBeau's on his way. Get out of there, or let me in."

Silence. She might be in the bathroom.

"Okay, for God's sake stay put and keep quiet. I'll come back when he's gone."

Clete had ducked into the stairwell just as the elevator door creaked open. He watched Jackie bang and yell until he pissed off people up and down the hall. Clete almost felt sorry for the little bastard.

When LeBeau gave up and left, Clete tried the door again himself. She had to be in there. The same apoplectic heads popped out. Finally he stood quiet, ear against the door. It was a full five minutes before he admitted to himself she was gone.

So he went to the Leopard, where Frank was supposed to phone him sometime after midnight. When the call came Marga brought a plug-in extension to his table.

"Clete?"

"Yeah, Frank?"

"Your girlfriend showed up around seven. Some old dame dropped her off. How'd you let her get away?"

"Never mind about that. She still there?"

"Yeah, I don't think she'll come out tonight. Just a hunch, I could be wrong. I took a chance to phone you, I'm in a booth a couple of blocks away."

"Think I should come over?"

"Hell, no. Get some rest. Come in the morning."

"I'll be there at six."

"Damn it, there's no sense coming that early. Make it nine o'clock. And sleep, don't go messing around with Marga. You're wound up tighter than some nose candy freak, if you don't chill down you'll get one of those damn headaches of yours. You'll be a hell of a lot of use outmaneuvering Octavian if you're laid out like a zombie in some dark room."

"Okay. Nine it is. Watch your ass tonight, Frank."

"Don't I always? See you."

Clete laid back in the chair and moaned. Damned prophet, Frank.

He'd had every intention of going on over there at six o'clock, but he didn't get to bed until four. Because he didn't take Frank's advice about Marga.

Well, he was tired of fending her off. After all, he wasn't celibate. That body of hers was German velvet, thick and thin in all the right places. And passionate? Whew. Made him forget about tall, skinny redheads for a while.

He'd anticipated the phone so long that when it finally rang it seemed like an hallucination. He catapulted up the hall and grabbed the receiver.

"Frank?"

"Am I getting overtime for this?"

"Nobody loves a smartass. Where are you?"

"Lobby of an inn in a village called Langenbruck. This has to be fast, the women are leaving."

"Women?"

"Hanna and some smart-looking older babe. They left Stillestrasse a few minutes past eight. Hanna hid when the car came out of the gate, but I knew damn well she was in there. Her head popped up after a couple of blocks."

"They on to you?"

"No. Unless they're damn good actresses."

"Hanna's wary though, if she made herself invisible when they left the house. Any idea where they're going?"

"A chalet, somewhere in the mountains. They ate lunch here, I eavesdropped."

"Have you seen Octavian or his flunkies?"

"LeBeau, Hippo, and the other guy broke into the place last night. I saw them go in and out. They made it without getting caught, but I'm sure they didn't get the triptych. They hung around the rest of the night, I saw the Mercedes a couple of times. They didn't follow up here."

"Must have bought Hanna's trick. Wonder how long it'll take them to know they've been had. Any idea who the other woman is?"

"Hanna called her Helene, the waiter knew her as Madame Mercier. They're headed out the door, Clete."

"I'm coming up there. Is that the only inn?"

"Yeah, you can't miss it."

"Stay with them until they get to the chalet. If it looks like they'll be there awhile go back to the inn. I'll meet you there. If you get tied up, try to call and leave a message. What're they driving?"

"Late model yellow BMW sedan. See you."

Clete took a map from his attaché case and found Langenbruck. He traced the route with his finger, then stripped and snaked into long underwear and ski pants.

He began to pile things on the bed.

Who was Helene Mercier? Bonnard family, he'd bet. If the waiter knew her the chalet was probably hers. Maybe the triptych was there. Or else they had it with them and wanted to lay low for a while.

He pulled on sheepskin-lined boots, buckled his shoulder holster, and grabbed an insulated white ski-trooper parka; everything else was in a backpack stowed in the car trunk.

On the front steps he almost collided with Frau Klein, the concierge. She had a shopping bag over one arm, the other was loaded with packages wrapped in brown paper.

"Hannalaure, just the woman I want. Frank's not here and I'm leaving. Don't know when we'll be back. If anyone asks. . . ."

Her black eyes were knowing. "If any person asks, I never heard of you."

"Thanks, *Liebchen*."

Clete threw the ski parka on the passenger seat and nosed the Saab into afternoon traffic with expert impatience, heading toward the Langenbruck road.

His headache was gone.

T·W·E·N·T·Y

THE box radiated importance. Lavishly carved from teak, the dust acquired during years of neglect couldn't hide a sheen achieved by generations of reverent care. There was a crude envelope attached to the lid with drops of candle wax that had spilled over into deep crevasses in the carving.

"What's this?" Hanna asked, moving aside for Helene to inspect the yellowed rectangle. Helene pulled a leather case out of her sweater pocket and extracted the small, silver-framed reading glasses. "It is old . . . directed to Ilse, but the envelope had been used before. Look there, an address was crossed out. I can make out part of it . . . a Russian address. Open it, *cherie*."

With extreme delicacy Hanna pulled the crumbling paper loose. The flap had been unsealed, she removed two sheets of paper that had been torn from a ledger book and pressed into service as stationery. They were covered with faded, shaky writing. She gave it to Helene.

"It's written in French. Can you read it?"

Helene unfolded the paper, smoothed it against the table and began to translate slowly.

Lura Livorna—9 April, 1917

My Dearest Ilse,

If by some miracle you receive this letter, you will know immediately from these poor writing materials how my life has been altered.

Or rather, it is no life at all.

God help me, Ilse. Petra is dead.

I have managed to write the words I have not yet spoken aloud, that was the hardest part. Now I will try to tell what happened in some kind of order.

The rebellion was everywhere. At first Petra believed I would be safer here in the country, then he changed his mind and decided to take me to Petrograd, to the Winter Palace. He came for me, and we spent three precious days together in a fragile bubble of happiness.

The pinprick came in the form of a messenger, a Corporal Lensky who had served under Petra on the German Front. He told us there was a sizable Bolshevik army (if one can call such rabble an army) that had come together in a small village twelve kilometers from here.

Tsarist troops were camped across the river from the Bolsheviks, under the command of Colonel Vasilova. They were badly outnumbered, and their commander so disabled by dysentery he could hardly sit up.

Petra prepared to leave immediately, I did not protest. Not out of optimism or bravery, but because my words would have been wasted.

Ilse, I sent him off with a kiss and a smile, as if he were going for an afternoon canter on his favorite horse. I never saw him again.

It was two days before we heard what happened. Corporal

Lensky, who had brought the first message, returned. He was filthy. His right hand wore a bloody bandage, he had lost two fingers in the battle. I ordered wine and the best of what food we had, and he told his story.

The way he described Petra in action, Ilse, it would have made you proud! He was everywhere on the battlefield, shouting encouragement to the cold, hungry, desperate troops. He told them how pleased the Tsar was with them, how well they would be rewarded when the rebellion was crushed.

The Bolsheviks were like ghosts, like creatures from the underworld. Silent men, poorly armed, many barefoot, they fought with grim determination.

Petra's death was quick, the corporal said. Someone called his name, he turned. His skull was split with an axe. Oh, God, Ilse, an axe!

When the Bolsheviks came to Lura Livorna three days later, I did not really care. They made our beautiful home into a military field hospital. The great parlor, the ballroom, the children's bedrooms; everywhere are moaning, screaming men and the stench of gangrene.

And now I am one of the patients.

In the beginning, the doctor in charge forced me to wear peasant's clothes and nurse the wounded. I worked eighteen hours a day, until I dropped into my bed too tired to undress. Or to think, and that was a blessing.

I came down with influenza. To be fair, they have done everything for me that they could. There are no medical supplies, and not very much food. I have no desire to get well. I welcome death, and a chance to join my beloved Petra.

That is all I have to tell. Now, as ever, I come to you asking favors.

My mind is at rest about Madeleine, I know you will raise her as your own daughter; it is Demi I worry about. As you know, Paul Anders, an American merchant whom Petra had befriended, took our dearest little Dimitri to the United States to live in a place called Philadelphia, Pennsylvania.

I am sure Mr. Anders is a good man, Ilse, but I do not really know anything about him, or the way that Americans live. Please, please, if you love me, go after Demi somehow and take him to live with you and his sister. Poor little lambs, they ought to be together.

About the box I sent with you. Please do not open it yet, unless for some reason you need money. There is an object inside of great worth, but it might cause you trouble until some time has passed.

If you do need money, (for a trip to America, or whatever) and must open the box, let no one into your confidence. No one. Leave the large object inside. There are a handful of rather fine loose stones that you can easily sell without attracting attention. Take them, and seal the box again. When the children are grown, Demi can decide what to do about the other thing. With your advice, of course.

You notice I have not considered the possibility you might have already opened it? I know you, my dearest friend, you have not.

I must mention one more thing, and ask absolution. It was never spoken between us, but I was aware that you loved Petra. I took him from you. I could not help myself, I loved him too, but that is no excuse.

You have been a perfect friend since the day we met, and I have been a bad one. Know that I love you better than anyone, except for Petra and my darling children. You are a generous woman, Ilse. Forgive me.

I lie now in a corner of the grand ballroom, curtained away from everyone else. I have not eaten in several days, they know I will die soon. Sometimes I am delirious, and imagine I am attending a great party. My dress is exquisite, a gown I bought in Paris. I dance with Petra, and everyone is jealous . . .

Oh, Ilse, pray for me. Pray for me.

Helene's voice was unsteady as she translated the final words. The silver-rimmed glasses had frosted over, she took them off and wiped her eyes. "Poor Ilse. She could not go after Demi, I expect. Kaiser Wilhelm had all Europe stirred to the boiling point with the first Great War. Ilse had defied her parents by going to Russia that last time and bringing Madeleine home, she would not have thought it right to upset them again by taking off to the United States. And then after the war . . . ah, who knows? Perhaps she thought she couldn't find him. So much time had passed."

"And when my Dedushka, Lisanne's 'dearest Demi,' did come to Switzerland, he was a man who had grown up to be an American. He came to take his sister away, not stay here with her," Hanna mused.

"Wars are full of heartbreak, *cherie*. No one was to blame."

Hanna nodded. "That's true. At least the letter has made me understand Lisanne a little better. She was spoiled and pampered, but not heartless. In the end she realized some of her own shortcomings."

Helene nodded. "Perhaps she was a better friend than you give her credit for. She certainly made Ilse's life interesting."

As they continued to speculate about Ilse and Lisanne, Hanna admired the box. Incised on the surface were figures of Mandarin lords and ladies strolling on a garden path. There was a little peak-roofed bridge over a stream that bore floating lotus flowers, other exotic blossoms lined the walk and weaved their way between delicate clumps of bamboo.

She guessed the coffer would measure twelve by sixteen inches, with a depth of perhaps ten inches. A thick band of sealing wax the color of dried blood girded the lid. In the center front was a round seal imprinted with the Romanov insignia.

"Ah, but that is enough talk of the past, *cherie*. Open it." Helene took a knife from a drawer under the table. "Here, to pry off the top."

First Hanna inserted the knife point under the seal's edge. It popped off easily. The band of wax embedded in the crack where the upper and lower portions intersected took longer; she rotated the box, working her blade.

Helene watched with barely contained impatience. After several minutes, when the table was littered with rusty shavings, Hanna felt the lid give.

"Hold the base firm, will you, please?"

Helene gripped the sides as Hanna eased the sections apart. A pleasant, pungent odor escaped. "Camphor. The box is lined with camphor wood."

A photograph lay on top, depicting a family in Edwardian clothes posed in a garden. The woman, in a white dress and wide-brimmed hat, knelt beside a little girl. A small boy stood between his parents, dressed in a sailor suit. He was looking up at his father. A spaniel flopped at the boy's feet, grinning, tongue out.

"It has to be Lisanne, Petra, and the children. They look as though they don't have a care in the world." She handed the picture to Helene.

Underneath was another envelope, this time of beautiful parchment scrawled in sepia ink. The flap was sealed with a blob of the red-brown wax, it was addressed simply to "Madeleine, from Mama." "Shall we save it for later?" Hanna asked.

Helene nodded and Hanna put the envelope aside.

The next article was heavy and rectangular, wrapped in folds of fringed ivory silk that was stiff with embroidered flowering vines. Gold threads gleamed in the design.

Helene was breathing audibly. Her cheeks were flushed, her lips slightly parted.

"A book, maybe?" Hanna guessed as she lifted it. "A family Bible, or photograph album?" Whatever the fabric protected was heavy. She set it on the table, the silken shroud fell away.

Revealed was a rectangle of translucent pink enamel, overlaying an engraved sunburst field. It was trellised with lines of rose diamonds, and edged with continuous green-gold laurel leaf borders. A diamond-studded gold medallion filled the central panel, crowned by a huge cabochon ruby.

Helene loosed a torrent of French, her admiration unmistakable. She put out a finger and touched the ruby.

"Oh, what *is* this?" Hanna asked, lifting the beautiful object with reverence. Hinged panels unfolded, revealing three small paintings. In the center was the Madonna and Child, brightly colored, rendered in almost primitive style. The Lady held her Babe and smiled beatifically. Her halo was a linked series of stars, behind her head gleamed a bright cerulean sky, dotted with smaller stars. Around the Babe's head was a gold circlet.

Both flanking paintings were versions of the Child, each faced inward. On the left an exquisitely brushed head of a boy of two or three, the halo behind his curls like a tilted hat. The colors were soft pastels. On the right was a chiaroscuro head of a baby, his halo a narrow golden band.

It was clear the three paintings were very old, and by different artists. Each was an exquisite example of its style, but they were overshadowed by the splendor of their setting.

Hanna refolded the piece. It was hinged so that, when closed, front and back were identical.

"It's a triptych, a religious icon," Helene said. "Look at the workmanship. Incredible. The way the panels fit together, I have never seen one done in that manner.

"And the engraving, the enamel work, the jewels. Unless I am very mistaken, this is the work of Carl Fabergé. Valuable; oh, I cannot begin to imagine. I see why Lisanne was concerned. Your grandfather did not exaggerate, Hanna. One could never dream of such a splendid thing."

Hanna was dazed. "This glorious work of art, hidden so long. He should have told someone. It belongs in a museum."

"You will give it up?" Helene asked with wonder. "But of course, you would want to sell it. Yes, that is wisest. You will be rich for the rest of your life."

"Sell it? Oh, I can't think. This can't be true. Fabergé. This is a piece of history, it doesn't belong to me." Her mind seethed with possibilities, one of them alarming. "It's not going back to Russia. Not if I can help it."

"You must have wise counsel, and time to make a decision." Helene's hands flew in an eloquent gesture. "We will put it in a bank vault in Basel, then secure the services of a lawyer and an expert on artifacts. I have excellent sources. Until that time, it would be best not to mention this triptych to anyone."

"Good advice."

There was something more in the box. Hanna picked up a small chamois bag.

"What's this, the jewels Lisanne mentioned?"

She pulled the bag open and poured its contents into her palm. A dozen or more stones lay there; red, green, purple. A sprinkle of diamonds, cut like teardrops, stood out among them. All were large.

"Mon Dieu."

Hanna spilled them from hand to hand. "I suppose they are quite valuable, but after the triptych they're anticlimactic."

When there was no answering comment Hanna looked up. Something had distracted Helene, she was facing the common wall between the kitchen and sitting room. A frown made vertical tracks between her eyes, she put cautioning fingers to her lips. "Hush. Do you not hear it?"

Hanna became aware of noise she had been too absorbed to notice, someone was hammering the front door with heavy, deliberate blows. Helene got up to investigate.

"Wait, don't go. Something's fishy, this isn't a night for drop-in guests. There's a blizzard going on out there."

But Helene was already out of the room. Hanna stuffed the triptych, jewels, picture, and letters into the box and looked wildly for a hiding place.

Where can I put it? Oh, damn, there's no place. Where, where? The room under the stairs?

Too easy for them to find.

Who were "they"?

Hanna didn't know, but she had a sick feeling she was going to find out. She jumped up with the box in her arms, slamming her sore knee against a chair.

My knee . . . the warming oven! Maybe I can get it open. . . .

She crossed the floor to the fireplace in three giant strides, knelt, and set the box on the hearth. Grasping the iron ring she pulled with all her strength, aided by the blast of adrenaline that raced through her body. The ring yielded. A rectangle opened in the wall, throwing out a cloud of soot.

Hanna shoved in the box and slammed the oven. She ran to the sink and sloshed water on her hands, arms, and face, wiping them on a cloth snatched from the table as she dashed after Helene. She dropped the cloth in the cloakroom under the stairs and burst into the sitting room.

Helene was at the door, her hand reaching for the bolt.

The banging stopped, A wavering voice called, "Madame, *c'est moi*, Cici."

Cici all right, but something was wrong.

"Please wait, Helene. For God's sake, what could make a lone girl come up the mountain on a night like this?" Hanna ran to a window and lifted a curtain. Clouds obscured the moon, but bright snow made several figures clearly visible.

"Get back, don't open it!"

Too late. The bolt slid free. Cici catapulted against her mistress, they fell in a heap of arms and legs at the bottom of the stair. As Hanna ran to their assistance four men streamed in. One was bloody, his hands tied behind his back. A giant wearing a red and black ski mask shoved him along with vicious force.

The other two Hanna recognized. Jackie LeBeau and the fur-coated man she had sketched in Geneva.

Hanna's jaw went slack. Jackie didn't surprise her, she had suspected he was a phony even before Clete's warning, now she cursed the misguided sympathy that had trapped her into being civil. But Fur-coat. Jackie sure hadn't been with him in Geneva, when had they joined forces? And the man with blood all over him, who the hell was he?

She began a protest, a challenge. The words died. Jackie had a gun.

Not a pistol; a heart-stopping thing that only existed in movies about revolutionaries or drug smugglers. He motioned with the barrel. "Get over there and sit, take the old sow with you. Now."

Hanna bent over Helene. Cici had scrambled off the floor, she was crouched like a small cat half up the stairs.

"Come on, Helene, we'd better do what he says."

A firm hand pushed her away, tension crackled in the room. With dignity expressed in every movement Helene stood and walked unassisted to a chair, her shoulders telegraphing anger. Hanna followed.

She heard footsteps on the stairs, a slap, a cry. Cici skittered to sit on the floor, huddled close to the dying fire. Each breath she took was a hiccuping sob.

Helene spoke, her control astonishing Hanna. "If you are kidnappers, you will be disappointed. There is no one with authority to disburse money for me, and Hanna is not wealthy."

"They didn't come after you, Helene. This is about the . . . this concerns me. I tried to warn you in Basel—"

"Silence! Keep your mouth shut, except to answer my questions." Fur-coat's voice had a theatrical quality, the plummy, clearly enunciated syllables were more menacing than a shout.

Something cold touched Hanna's chin. She flinched. Jackie's gun slid up her cheek, ending with the barrel pressed against her temple.

"Bang!" he yelled, and laughed.

"Not yet, Jackie. Miss Anders has something to tell us.

"Miss Anders . . . I may call you Hanna? Hanna, Jackie dislikes you. I might say without fear of exaggeration, he dislikes you violently. I will try to restrain him, but . . ." Fur-coat shrugged.

"Why, Jackie? Why hate me? I haven't done anything to you. God knows I was patient . . ." Hanna stopped, humiliated.

I sound like an hysterical fool. Damned if I plead for mercy from a craven little poseur like Jackie LeBeau.

"Bitch, I'll tell you—" Jackie broke off at the sound of a scuffle. The ski-masked monster was slapping his prisoner. As Hanna watched he shoved the man to the floor and gut-kicked him. The man jackknifed, spitting blood and curses.

The monster peeled off his mask to reveal a brutish, leering face. "We've got the women, let me finish Rivera."

"Leave him, Hippolyte. Not until we know what Cross is up to. Go outside, tell Dieter I said for him to guard the rear. You stay out in front."

Hippolyte's hands opened and closed. He looked at the still figure on the floor.

"Get out of here." Fur-coat's voice was deadly velvet. "Don't take your eyes off the entrance. Do you understand?"

Hippolyte grunted and lumbered out.

After the door closed Jackie sniggered. "We'll toss out a chunk of raw meat, if you're a good boy."

He looked at Fur-coat. "That's a dangerous beast, Octavian. One day you won't be able to control him."

"Speak for yourself, Jackie. I control him well enough. Hippolyte is useful, within certain parameters. His fear of me is greater than his desire to run amok. If that changes, he will not live to regret it."

He turned to Hanna. "You had better hope I don't loose the Hippo on you again. Cross isn't here to play hero. Or is he?"

"It was that unspeakable oaf who assaulted me? . . . This is madness. You won't get away with it."

"Be silent! You are a foolish woman. Why did you goad me in the Geneva station, waving that portrait in my face? No one knew you existed until then. Surely you didn't mean to warn me off by displaying your knowledge of my presence? You can't be that much of a fool."

"Who the hell *are* you, Mr. . . . Octavian . . . is that what Jackie called you? Idi Amin resurrected, in grease paint and lynx? How would you expect a woman from Denver, Colorado, on her first trip abroad, to recognize you? I'd never have noticed you at all if it hadn't been for that ridiculous coat. I had a few minutes, you have an interesting face. I'm an artist, making pictures is what I do. It's that simple."

"I warn you not to persist in this charade." He stood over her, so close Hanna was forced to tilt her head at an awkward angle.

"Two things only I want from you. Where is the triptych and where is Cross?"

"How can you know about the triptych? It's been hidden away for seventy years."

His palm exploded against her cheek. She hadn't seen it coming, her neck popped with the violence of the blow. She tasted blood, the side of her face went numb. She reached up to touch it.

"Try again. Where is the triptych and where is Cross? Think before you answer."

Hanna looked at her fingers. They were bloody from the cut on her mouth. "You are insane," she whispered.

Helene intervened. "Monsieur Octavian, she has no idea where the triptych is, nor do I. My aunt disposed of it many years ago. The proceeds were used to feed and educate Hanna's great-aunt, Madeleine Anderson." She darted a glance at Hanna, who mouthed the words, "I hid it."

Octavian's response was a surprise. "You cannot even tell the same lies. Well, it looks as though we shall have a long night. Come along, ladies, to the kitchen. Jackie, bring Rivera." He sounded almost jovial.

"Wait!" He wrenched Hanna's arm. "Are you planning a little surprise for us? Do you have Cross concealed in the house, perhaps in the kitchen? We caught his friend napping outside."

"What's the matter, you two have a misunderstanding? So

much for honor among thieves," Hanna jeered. "If Clete Cross is around it's news to me. You know more about him than I do."

Octavian lifted a twin to Jackie's gun and held it against Hanna's rib cage. He attempted to encircle her throat with his free arm. He couldn't do it, had to settle for a vicious grip on the back of her neck. Hanna suppressed the desire to giggle.

A disturbance erupted behind, something heavy and metallic crashed to the floor.

"Rivera, you stupid sonofabitch. What were you gonna do with fire tongs? You're trussed like a chicken. Wasn't Hippo's lesson enough for you? One more stunt and it'll be your bloody damn carcass we throw to him."

"Untie me, LeBeau, my nose itches."

"Maybe I'll blow it off, save you the trouble of scratching."

"Come on, Jackie, don't let him bait you." Octavian was impatient, he prodded Hanna. She started off, under the stairs, through the dining room, and into the kitchen. Helene followed with Cici clinging to her. Jackie was last, shoving Rivera in front.

"Put them in chairs. Tear that cloth on the table into strips and tie their arms behind. All but the little Cici; I have use for her."

Jackie pushed Frank down, Octavian released Hanna, she sat beside Helene. Cici backed to the wall beside the refrigerator, her eyes like a sleepwalker's.

"Move your chairs away from the table," Octavian said. He pointed to an area in front of the sink. "There."

Jackie picked up one of the linen tablecloths and tore it into serviceable lengths. He tied Helene first, then Hanna, pulling her arms behind the chair rungs and knotting the bonds with vicious jerks.

"You snotty bitch. Made me puke, acting like I had the hots for you. Nobody walks out on Jackie LeBeau. You think about that."

He finished tying her and flipped her head up with a slap under the chin. "Look at me, bitch."

Hanna obeyed, trying to keep her face impassive.

Jackie smiled. "Ah, but I've got a tender heart, ask anyone.

You be working on an apology. If you beg hard enough, I might let you out of here alive." He caressed Hanna's cheek, her neck, cupped a breast. He pinched.

"Stop it!" Octavian's voice was shrill with fury. Jackie jumped back in surprise.

"Don't waste your time, Jackie. We have much to do." The cultured voice was back to normal. "Are your prisoners secure? Then I suggest we discuss procedure.

"I have decided to bring the helicopter in from across the border. You did observe a landing pad beside the house? Most convenient."

"A helicopter, in this weather?" Jackie was too alarmed to resist questioning his leader's judgment.

"Tomorrow, at daybreak. The weather is forecast to clear during the night."

"Oh. Well, yeah, that should work, as long as this crap moves on over the mountains. But we don't have the triptych yet." He jerked a thumb at the prisoners. "And what about them, we can't take the whole bunch of 'em along."

"We will have it in our possession before we leave, I am convinced it is here. As for these scraps of humanity. . . ." He cocked his head and placed a finger against his lips, miming consideration. "Four of us, a pilot and copilot. High altitude flying, too, across the Alps. Ah, you're right, Jackie. We can take one, at most. Perhaps that will be the person who tells us where the triptych is. As for the others. . . ." He shook his head in mock regret. "We shall see when the time comes."

Octavian walked to the kitchen telephone and lifted it. He held it out toward Cici and asked, "Is this the only telephone?"

Cici whimpered.

He advanced on the terrified girl. "You're very frightened, aren't you, little one? That's because you're smart enough to recognize danger, and show respect. Now, is there another of these? Another telephone?"

Comprehension brought an eager nod. *"Oui."* She pointed to the ceiling. "Up there."

"Good." He ripped the cord from the wall, dropped the instrument, and kicked it across the room.

"Now, Mademoiselle Cici, fix Monsieur LeBeau and me something hot to drink, there's a good girl. And food, I'm sure there are supplies here, whatever you can find. Bring them upstairs, *comprendez-vous?*"

Cici nodded.

"Be quick, or I'll send Monsieur LeBeau to fetch you. You wouldn't like that, would you?"

Cici's head shook in a violent negative.

Octavian addressed the man they had called Rivera. "We'll have our chat very soon. I advise you to change your attitude and tell us where Cross is, I don't like surprises."

Hanna suspected he was saving the real chiller for Helene and her. The instinct was correct, except she hadn't expected physical violence. Octavian approached Helene, the genial expression once again in place.

Helene watched him, her chin lifted in defiance.

"Where is the triptych, Madame?"

"I told you, my aunt sold it decades ago."

Octavian began to slap her, one violent, sickening blow after another. Hanna screamed, "Stop it." Rivera cursed, his voice rising above Jackie's laughter.

Helene made no sound at all, she took the clouts chin lifted, staring at Octavian with contempt. It became a contest of wills. Octavian's control snapped, one final, closed-fist blow sent her reeling, her head bounced to the side and stayed there.

"Goddamn, Octavian, you've killed her. We don't have the triptych yet," Jackie bleated.

Octavian stood splay-legged, breathing hard. He lifted Helene's head by her hair and let it drop again. "She's not dead. Besides, Hanna knows where the triptych is hidden, don't you, my dear? Think about what happened to your friend, while Jackie and I are absent." He started for the door.

"Jackie? Come along, we must make arrangements for the helicopter."

"Right, half a second." He advanced to Hanna. "I never did make it with an amazon. You have something to look forward to. Me, Dieter, and the Hippo, we'll stake you on a bed, just before dawn. Rivera can watch, and your friend there, if she's still alive." He lifted the gun. Then, "BAM! BAM! BAM! You all go together."

"Jackie!" Octavian was coming back through the door. Jackie scuttled.

T·W·E·N·T·Y-O·N·E

CLETE'S rental Saab lurched and skidded up the snow-covered road. Whirling flakes rushed at the windshield and were swept to either side like water flowing around a rock. Clete squinted. The continuous motion played tricks on his eyes, he felt the beginnings of vertigo and forced himself to focus on something inside the car.

His fingers ached from clutching the wheel. He flexed them, and gritted his teeth as the sudden flow of blood trebled the pain.

It seemed hours since he had left Basel. The storm had increased to a blinding fury; the road was almost lost in a shifting gray sea. Suddenly, at the apex of its fury, the wind died, as if he were in the eye of a hurricane. The snow slacked off, dark shapes and flickers of light teased his vision. Langenbruck.

He pushed through the door of the inn, found a seat in the dining room and ordered coffee. When it was served he picked up his cup and strolled back to the main room. He stood by the fire, reached for cigarettes, and put them back with an oath of irritation, then wandered, looking at photographs and mementoes on the walls.

Frank hadn't made it back.

Clete walked to the desk and struck up a conversation with the innkeeper.

"Vicious storm. Kind of early in the season, isn't it?"

The man looked up from his ledger. "No, the roads have been closed earlier than this. You are American, I know the American accent from my army days. You have traveled in the Alps before?"

"Yes, but not here, and not in late October. I've always come in summer, or else around Christmas for skiing."

The innkeeper abandoned his ledger and came to the counter. He was tall and lean, with a clipped gray mustache and shrewd, steel-blue eyes.

"You are not a guest here, are you?"

"No, I'm just passing through."

"The plows will be out tomorrow. If the snow stops, the main roads will be open by evening. You had best stay with us tonight, we will make room for you."

Clete set his coffee cup on the desk. "I wish I could, but I have to find someone and deliver an emergency message. I thought you might be able to help me."

The man shook his head. "You cannot go farther until tomorrow. Stay here." He seemed irritated by Clete's stupidity.

Clete made a pretense of looking tempted. "I wish that were possible, but I'm afraid not. Let me tell you the situation, then you'll understand why I have to make a stab at it.

"I'm looking for a young woman named Hanna Anders, a friend of mine. I came to Basel a month ago, transferred from my home office in New York. I'd just met Hanna and I really liked her, so I talked her into coming for a visit."

"Yes?"

"It worked out fine. She's staying with a Swiss woman, a friend of her mother's. A Madame Mercier, who used to run a school in Basel. They left this morning on a trip to the Mercier woman's chalet. Up here, somewhere."

The innkeeper nodded impatiently. “I am acquainted with Frau Mercier. She came through here at midday with a tall young woman. They stopped for a meal.”

“Oh, good, you saw them.”

“So what is the emergency?”

“I didn’t tell you that part? Sorry.

“I got a call from the States around noon, it was the friend who introduced Hanna and me. She was frantic, couldn’t reach Hanna.

“Her brother, Hanna’s that is, was killed in a motorcycle accident last night. Horrible thing. They were very close. Their parents are dead, no other children. Hanna will be devastated.”

The innkeeper broke in. “That is a tragedy, but I know how to solve your problem. Madame Mercier has a telephone at her chalet, I have the number. You should be able to contact them, unless the lines are down.”

Clete appeared to make an agonizing decision. He shook his head. “No, I can’t give her the news that way. It’s too impersonal. I’ve got to tell her face to face.

“The storm’s let up, it stopped snowing before I came in. And I’ve got a borrowed Saab, it’s a good mountain car. I have to go on. Will you give me directions?”

“I have seen storms in these Alps all my life, and I say to you we will have more from this one before the night is over. I will draw you a map, but you are a fool to risk it.”

Clete affected an overconfident grin. “I feel like a lucky fool, tonight. One other thing, I brought a thermos. Could I have it filled with coffee from your kitchen?”

The innkeeper nodded. “Anna?” he raised his voice.

A short, sweet-faced woman appeared. Clete handed her the thermos and made his request.

Ten minutes later he had instructions and a supply of coffee. He needed to know one more thing, and framed a careful question in his head. It wouldn’t do to make the innkeeper suspicious, he might phone the chalet to warn Madame Mercier as soon as the strange American walked out the door.

"You've been very helpful. I don't think I introduced myself. Clete Cross. I really do appreciate your help, sir." He pulled a twenty-franc note out of his money clip and offered it.

The man waved it off. "No, no. Keep your money. Before the night is over you will curse me for letting you go."

Clete reached out, grasped the man's hand in a firm shake. "Well, sir, I hope you're wrong. Thanks again."

He started off, snapped his fingers, and turned.

"Oh, by the way. Did a man named Frank Rivera leave a message for me?"

"Message? I know of none. Frank Rivera, you say? Why would he leave a message here?"

"It's not important. Something to do with my business. I left word I was coming this way, if he needed to contact me. But if you're sure. . . ."

"No one has left a message for you, Mr. Cross."

"Good-bye, then. I'll be bringing Hanna back tomorrow, maybe we can stop for something to eat. If not, I'd like to come another time, stay a few days. I like your inn very much."

As he crossed the long, comfortable room he heard a song begin from the dining room. First one voice, then several, blending in a robust drinking ballad.

In front of him was a single couple, aloof from the merrymaking. They sat on the sofa by the hearth, arms around each other.

The girl looked up as Clete passed. A redhead. He smiled and she winked; her lover frowned and pulled her lips to his.

Clete opened the door and was repossessed by the cold, glittering darkness.

T·W·E·N·T·Y-T·W·O

HELENE, do you hear me? Oh, damn it, please, Helene. Say something."

No response, no movement. No change in the sickening sideways angle of the head above the limp, slender body.

"Cici, help Madame Mercier. Untie her arms, wet a rag with cold water and hold it against her forehead. Cici, you little coward, she'll die if you don't do something."

Cici refused to hear. She scurried around the kitchen, pulled things from cabinets, and poured water into a teapot.

"Then cut me loose, I'll help her. You can't mean to let her die."

"No use, Hanna, the girl's terrified. You're making it worse, name-calling. Give her time to calm down, then I'll talk to her."

"Oh, you're a psychologist? What are you doing here, anyway, Mr. Rivera? Clete too busy to come steal the triptych himself?"

"Clete will be along. He's my friend. I also happen to work for him. And we have every right to be here, we represent the legal owner of the triptych."

Hanna sputtered, between a laugh and a jeer. "Oh, right! I believe that. Were Helene and I the only people in the world who didn't know the triptych existed until today? Was it written up in the Sunday *Times*, or something?"

"We're in a hell of a spot, Hanna, and I'm in a foul mood. Cut the crap, will you?"

On the verge of another nasty remark, Hanna stopped to think. Madeleine Anderson had died somewhere around two weeks ago. Had the woman in Madeleine's apartment mentioned a will? Hanna couldn't remember, but suppose she bequeathed the triptych to someone other than family. If that were true, Clete and this man Rivera might be legitimate.

If they came to Basel representing a legatee at the same time I got here . . . dear God, what a coincidence. Is it possible?

"Mr. Rivera, I'll assume you're telling the truth. Would you mind giving this mysterious employer of yours a name? I'm fascinated in how he or she became the 'legal owner' of the triptych."

"Name's Frank. My name, that is. Are you on the level? You don't know about the will?"

"Frank, as you pointed out, this is no time for games.

"My grandfather was Madeleine Anderson's brother. I assume you know who she is, since you mention a will.

"From the time he came to live with us in Denver when I was a child, he told me I had an inheritance in Basel, left by his Russian family. I believed him, at least I wanted to. It gave the two of us a wonderful secret. My parents, if they heard him talk about it at all, thought he was senile.

"Anyway, I came to Europe a few months ago; and sure, I was going to check it out. Who wouldn't? I hadn't meant to do it now . . . that's beside the point.

"I don't know what I expected to find. Not anything like the triptych. It's beyond anyone's imagination."

Frank appeared to be judging the truth of her explanation.

"Okay, maybe you're legit. Madeleine Anderson left the

triptych to the Eastern Orthodox Church. She gave her parish priest the will years ago."

"The Church! Of course, that makes sense. But why hire you and Clete? Why not just send a priest over with a copy of the will, to pick the triptych up from Helene."

"It wasn't that easy. The will mentioned a woman named Ilse Bonnard, in Basel. Period. The priest remembered the old gal talking about a street, Stillestrasse. We'd have found the place, but you speeded things up. And caused us a hell of a lot of trouble."

"I caused you trouble! What about Octavian and Jackie? Where did they come from? You seem well acquainted."

Frank sighed. "It would take too long to explain. There'll be time for that later, when Clete gets here."

Hanna felt immense relief. "He knows where we are?"

"Not exactly, but he'll find us."

He looked at Cici. "I'm going to have a try at the girl."

Cici had gathered crackers, cheese, and tinned meat, and arranged them on a tray. Now she was measuring tea into a pot of steaming water with shaking hands.

"Cici, look at me." Frank's voice was gentle, persuasive.

The girl kept her eyes on the tea, but a soft answer came. "*Oui?*"

"I know how scared you are. You have a right." Frank turned to Hanna.

"Do you know how much English she understands?"

Hanna nodded. "She's pretty fluent; she has an American boyfriend. She had a hard time understanding Octavian because he frightened the wits out of her."

"Cici, it's okay to be afraid. I'm scared too. We're in a bad situation, all of us. Don't think they're not going to hurt you because they didn't tie you up. They'll use you and then kill you just like the rest of us. They can't afford to let anyone live."

A choked scream was Cici's answer. She stared at Frank, a hand across her mouth.

"Listen to me. Come here and cut me loose. Be a brave girl, it won't take a second. I'll look after you, I promise.

"Look at Madame Mercier. You like her, don't you? She's been good to you. She has to get to a doctor, fast. No one can help her but you."

Cici shook her head violently. "No, I will not listen. You cannot do anything. They will kill me for sure if I let you go."

She lifted the teapot onto her tray of food, clutched it against her waist and scurried out of the kitchen.

Hanna was furious. "There she goes, looking out for number one. If they don't murder her, I will."

Frank's words came back to her. "They really are going to kill us, aren't they? Even if I give them the triptych."

"So you do know where it is?" He shook his head. "For God's sake don't tell me.

"Listen, Hanna, don't let them have it. Clete's coming, he really is. Hold out as long as you can, because the minute they have the triptych they'll blow us all away."

Hanna had never felt such bleak terror in her life. She tried to answer, but her throat was paralyzed. She worked her mouth and tried again. "Is there any chance Clete will get here before they . . . ?"

"Sure there is. I can't count the times that boy's saved my ass. Of course, I've saved his once or twice, too."

Hanna looked at Helene. "Frank, what about her? Do you think—"

"Can you move your fingers?" he interrupted. "I'll work my chair around so our backs are together. Maybe one of us can help the other."

It almost worked. Hanna had picked loose a knot in the linen that tied Frank's hands when Jackie came in, followed by Octavian.

Jackie laughed. "You never quit, do you, Rivera? It couldn't have done you any good. When I tie someone they stay put."

Octavian interrupted, "Jackie, get the Hippo. I want his help with Rivera."

Jackie went out, Octavian opened the back door. Hanna felt an icy blast.

"Dieter, where are you? Hippo's coming in, go around to the front. You haven't seen anything?"

Hanna heard a garbled answer.

"All right. Keep your head up."

A complaint was forthcoming.

"I know how cold it is. When Hippolyte finishes with Rivera, you can come in and thaw out." He shut the door and advanced on Frank.

"Rivera, you will tell me where Cross is. Why don't you be good to yourself and do it now?"

"I can't tell what I don't know, you sonofabitch, even if that drooling piece of sewer sludge kills me."

Octavian patted his lips. The corners of his mouth twitched, he stared at Frank with an obscene look of anticipation. The scene held until Jackie came in with Hippolyte.

Hippo stomped snow off his boots. "Cross ain't out there, and won't be. No one can make it up here tonight." He walked to the fire and spat.

"Don't make rash assumptions. Cross is an obstinate man, and a devious one. He would love us to get careless," Octavian retorted.

"Then let me work on Rivera again."

"Precisely why I sent for you. Take him upstairs. Jackie, keep your gun ready."

Hanna watched Hippo untie Frank and lift him out of the chair with ham-sized fists.

Jackie winked at Hanna and said, "Your turn later, baby. Don't be impatient, we gotta learn where your boyfriend is, first. Octavian doesn't like interruptions." They left.

Helene coughed.

"Are you conscious? Please, talk to me," Hanna urged.

Helene didn't answer or move, only whimpering sounds came from her throat.

Hanna alternated between guilt, fury, and spiraling panic. If she'd stayed on Ibiza as she originally planned none of this would have happened.

Clete could still get here in time.

She looked at Helene. Maybe it was already too late.

T·W·E·N·T·Y-T·H·R·E·E

THE snow-packed road was alive. Deep, soft, voluptuous; it undulated under the wheels of the Saab like a lazy whore. The incline was steeper by the minute, Clete needed all his driving skill to keep the car close against the mountainside, away from the black abyss that yawned to his left. He worked the gears to relieve the straining engine.

The rush of confidence he had felt after his success in Langenbruck was gone, now apprehension raised terrible specters of what he might find when he got to the chalet. Frank, Hanna; if either of them were harmed it would be his fault. Madame Mercier, too.

Frank had wanted to pull out as soon as Octavian Demopolis showed up. That would have been the wisest thing, Clete knew. It was folly for two men to take on an organization like Octavian's.

Money and power, the most dangerous commodities on earth, in the hands of a megalomaniac.

Clete's eyes were watering, he pulled off a glove and swiped at them with the back of his hand. The Saab dipped to the left, he eased it back in the tracks.

Tracks. Three sets. Two half obscured, the third with a light sprinkle of powder. That was easy enough to read, Hanna and the Mercier woman first, then Frank, then . . . Octavian.

It didn't have to be Octavian. Maybe there was another chalet, someone else fool enough to fight his way up the mountain in a blizzard.

Sure.

Hanna. He could have warned her, laid his cards on the table at dinner that night. He had the perfect opening when she began to talk about her grandfather. He hadn't trusted her.

I tried to warn her about LeBeau.

Too late.

He knew he wasn't sane on the subject of Octavian. A one-sided feud, Octavian thought of him as a minor annoyance. A pesky fly that wouldn't light long enough to be swatted.

You sonofabitch, I've come a long way from the pink-cheeked Harvard kid you pushed around.

Hanna had seemed so vulnerable when she talked about her grandfather. Funny how grandfathers figured in this deal. His vendetta with Octavian had started with his own mother's father, a quintessential Bostonian who had owned a small, exclusive jewelry store almost two centuries old.

Clete smiled, thinking about Dad Talbot. They had started off bad. Clete had been determined to hate Boston; he figured to mark time until he was old enough to hightail it back to Sioux Falls and be a newspaper man, like his real dad.

What a pain in the butt he'd been. Rude, prickly, insufferable brat with a midwestern accent that must have grated on Dad Talbot's ears.

The old man hadn't been patronizing, though. He'd bided his time, until finally Clete began to be curious about the things in glass display cases in the library. "The Talbot Collection."

"Where did this come from? What's it made out of? How old is it?"

The old man had his opening. Like Hanna's grandfather, he could spin a hell of a yarn. He made Clete see the collection as more than rare and valuable, each piece manifested the need of a human being to express the aesthetic, the beautiful.

Clete forgot about being a reporter and began working in the jewelry store on Saturdays and during summer vacation. By the time he enrolled in college it was understood he'd take his place as the next Talbot in a business founded in 1794. Never mind his name was Cross, he was the only Talbot left. Nobody counted his mother, sunk into a state of maudlin alcoholism.

He'd had four years toward a Harvard MBA under his belt when the unthinkable happened. He would carry the picture in his mind until he died: A frail, old man in a maroon silk dressing gown, sprawled across the black and white marble foyer.

It was Christmas week. Clete had been to a fraternity party. He was just sober enough to execute the complicated pattern, disguised by figures carved in the door, that disengaged the burglar alarm.

The green light didn't come on. He went though the process again, no light. He jammed his key into the deadbolt and forced the door open. The alarm should have sounded off with a cacophony of ear-splitting shrieks. Nothing. Dead silence.

Even now the memory caused him to break out in a cold sweat. How many times had he relived it? The searing pain in his gut when he saw the pitiful body. The blood. The utter, stark despair of sinking to his knees and cradling the only human being he loved in his arms; pleading, crying, begging God to restore life where there was none.

The Clete who opened the door to the police was not the half-drunk fraternity boy who had fumbled his way into the house.

The Talbot Collection had vanished, of course. Clete's mother had been on one of her periodic hospital visits; the manservant who lived in was gone on holiday vacation. Leaving a fragile old man. Duck soup.

Clete haunted the two homicide detectives assigned to the case. They were tolerant. One, Sanderson, an old-young man with a sad face, was never too busy to spend a few minutes with Clete. Clete began to realize that the brutal murder enraged Len Sanderson as much as himself.

Len told him about Octavian. Len's own knowledge plus scraps picked up from informants pointed to one person, Octavian Demopolis. A wealthy man with criminal connections, Demopolis had access to people with the expertise to disarm a sophisticated burglar alarm. He was a collector and he was totally unscrupulous. He was also brilliant.

The most significant thing about the theft was the nature of the objects stolen. The Talbot Collection didn't consist of individual jewels or pieces set with large precious stones, easily disposed of. What made it unique was age, history, craftsmanship.

There were pomander jars of French enamel and gold, eighteenth-century Oriental snuff boxes, delicate necklaces of Egyptian glass, centuries old. Unique, traceable, impossible to sell.

That left Octavian. Rich, pseudo-respectable Greek shipping tycoon, owner of a fabulous collection of art objects.

Some pieces were on display in his Manhattan flat, some on loan to museums. A few people knew he had another collection, one that only Octavian himself had ever seen. No one knew where it was, no one could prove it existed. But they knew.

"That piece of excrement murdered your grandfather, Clete, but there's not a damn thing we can do about it. We can't touch him, neither can NYPD. Can't get inside his flat without a warrant, can't get a warrant without probable cause.

"Even if we could, there's no guarantee we'd find anything. His illegal things could be stashed anywhere in the world, he has homes in a dozen countries. We're screwed. Dead end."

"You're screwed, Len. I'm not."

Clete drove to the city that night. By noon the next day he knew where Octavian lived. He conned his way inside the building, handing out fifty-dollar bills and laying on the Harvard accent.

He got all the way to Octavian's door, where he made a noisy ass of himself. Two hired hands were disposing of him when Octavian himself appeared.

Clete spat threats and accusations. The man listened impassively, a slight smile twisting his lips. When he grew bored, he lifted a finger and crooked it at the waiting elevator. Ten minutes later Clete lay in the street beside a garbage can, battered senseless.

He joined the Army before they drafted him and went to 'Nam. Home in one piece, he exerted enough self-control to finish his MBA. He owed it to the old man.

The jewelry store was too much, though. It was sold to a middle-age widow, a Mrs. Gluck. No more "Talbot's."

He left Boston and put in his application with the New York City Police Department. A millionaire cop with an Ivy League degree, he got plenty of harassment. He weathered it, and in three and a half years made detective. With his background, he drifted into becoming the resident expert on objets d'art and jewels.

He fantasized arresting Octavian, it was an obsession. He even dreamed of the perfect frame. In the end, the best he could manage was nuisance value. He decided to be as maddening as the nut photographer who drove Jacqueline Onassis batty.

He made himself familiar with Octavian's top hoods, noting the rise of Jackie LeBeau with interest.

Frustrated and heading for trouble with the brass, he quit the force during his ninth year in the Department. He had been a lieutenant for three months.

Frank Rivera, a homicide sergeant, was his best friend since rookie days. A mixed-breed Hispanic born street-smart, Frank took Clete under his wing from the first. They became inseparable buddies. No one could figure it out. They had nothing in common.

When Clete left the Department, Frank went with him. They started a consultant business, dealing mostly with insurance companies.

By the time an Orthodox Church representative called for help in locating a Fabergé triptych in Switzerland, Clete had advanced to the point where he sometimes didn't think of Octavian Demopolis for days at a time.

That changed in a flash when he saw Octavian in the Geneva station. The whole thing was fresh in his mind, like it happened yesterday.

He had brushed aside Frank's concerns.

Had his treatment of Hanna really been fair, or had he been too preoccupied to use good judgment?

The Saab faltered, Clete looked at the fuel gauge. A quarter full. He had gas cans in the trunk, so that was all right.

If he had read the innkeeper's map correctly he was almost there. Time to shake off regrets and memories. Sure enough, as he rounded a curve he saw lights, and snuffed his own. The chalet.

His hand went to the 93R Beretta in its leather holster, then to clips of ammunition slung under the opposite arm. He backed around the curve and out of sight, then parked.

Outside the car, he opened the trunk and rummaged in his backpack, then pulled on a white ski mask. Easing the trunk shut, he melted into shadows at the edge of the road.

It wasn't a difficult climb, but he cursed the noise of his boots in crusty snow. The clouds had thickened again, this time the snow was big-deal serious. Flakes the size of half dollars dropped to the ground like plumb bobs.

When he got close to the chalet he crossed to the far side of the road, using sparse trees and outcroppings of rock for shelter. Lights streamed from the windows, upstairs and down. He saw a balcony on the second level, to his left as he faced the house.

There was someone out front; stamping, clapping hands to

keep the blood flowing. Making no attempt at concealment. Frank wouldn't be that careless, it had to be Octavian's man.

Where was Frank?

Clete moved on. He saw two cars in a parking area to the left of the house. One pale, the other dark. Hanna and Madame Mercier had come up in a yellow BMW, according to Frank. The other car, he could see now, was a black Mercedes.

There had to be a third car. Clete worked his way farther up the road. He wasn't much concerned about Octavian's guard, the dunce seemed too wrapped up in his own miseries to care if a UFO landed and little green men with pitchforks poured out.

Tired treads and footprints led around a hairpin curve, Clete followed. The road dwindled to nothing. At the very end was an automobile, driver's door gaping. Clete covered the distance running. He expected to see Frank's body sprawled across the seat.

It was Frank's Peugeot, all right, empty. The snow was churned in a ten-foot circle around the open door; the mess funneled downhill as if something had been dragged along the ground. There were smaller scuffle marks in a couple of spots.

Clete had an attack of the shakes, he leaned against the car. Frank was inside the house.

There was a good chance he was alive, Clete told himself. Octavian would want to know what Clete was up to before they offed Frank. Frank would hold out, he'd know he was a dead man the minute he coughed up the information.

Clete started back down toward the pleasant, welcoming facade of the chalet.

T·W·E·N·T·Y-F·O·U·R

THE last log in the fireplace collapsed inward, sending a brilliant shower of sparks. Hanna watched until the fireworks subsided into glowing cherry fragments. The room was cold, but that was the least of her problems.

She felt a compulsion to swallow. Her throat was corrugated like it had been flushed out with battery acid. Her eyes couldn't tear anymore, the lids felt like turgid, sticky caterpillars.

How long had it been since Frank was forced upstairs, leaving her alone? Worse than alone; Hanna couldn't stop watching Helene, wondering if she were dying.

What difference did it make? At least she was mercifully unconscious. They would all be dead soon.

That did it. Wallowing in bathos wasn't her style. She was still alive and more or less unscathed, and there was no time to waste on mindless panic; she might still be able to help herself and Helene.

Frank managed to move his chair before they came back and caught us. Maybe I can move this one.

If she could move . . . that would be something. She leaned

forward, tilting the chair on two legs. With slow, steady pressure she straightened her knees until the chair was completely off the floor. She inched along like a clumsy turtle.

Action pumped blood through numb arms and legs, the pain brought on a wave of nausea. She eased the chair to the floor.

So it hurts, but I can do it. Now. There has to be a rough surface somewhere that's not out of reach. Linen's strong, but not so tough friction won't wear it away.

She evaluated everything in the room, starting with the hearth. The stone exterior of the fireplace, maybe? No, there was a lip on the hearth, she might not be able to negotiate the rise. Try for something simpler.

She remembered the knife she'd used to open the Oriental box. What had happened to it? Hadn't she seen Jackie using it to rip the linen cloths? He would have disposed of it, he was too smart to leave it lying around.

There was something on the drain board beside the sink. A piece of cutlery? How much time did she have before they came back? She became obsessed with the need to hurry and scrambled too fast, losing control. The chair legs slammed to the floor.

She closed her eyes and murmured a half-forgotten prayer. Minutes passed, no one came.

An image came to her. Cici at the sink, sawing at a block of cheese. With a knife.

She crept this time, the chair riding her back like the shell of a hermit crab. At the cabinet she eased it to the floor and closed her eyes a few seconds until the pain subsided.

The knife lay with its handle toward her. She lunged her upper torso across the drainboard. Her body was in a terrible vise, the chair threatened to decapitate her, but she could touch the knife with her forehead. She tried to nudge it closer.

It pivoted out of reach. In a burst of fury she lunged again. Her head crashed against the lip of the sink and she fell to the left, her arm caught between chair and floor. Agony made a black whirlpool and spun her into oblivion.

Something chaffed, rubbed at her wrists. God, it hurt. She started to protest, a hard palm covered her mouth.

"Quiet! It's Clete."

She opened her eyes and saw she was on her back, free of the chair. Clete stood over her.

Was she hallucinating?

"Get up." The hallucination forced her to stand, his hands under her armpits. When she was on her feet he pushed her forward.

She stiffened and looked at Helene.

"Not now!"

She was being lifted into the window and shoved through like a sack of flour. A nail ripped her sweater and raked across her stomach. She gasped, then coughed as her lungs filled with frigid air.

His hands were on her thighs, shoving. She fell into ice-covered stalks of dead flowers.

Clete landed in a crouch, stood and pulled the casement shut. He squatted and whispered, "Come on, I can't carry you. Move!"

Clinging to the wall, they crept under the balcony to the rear of the chalet, then followed a granite bluff similar to the one across the road. They circled until they were in a stand of trees directly across the parking area from the kitchen window.

Clete stopped and patted her shoulder. "Okay, take it easy. Sorry I had to be rough."

Hanna sank to the ground.

"Don't do that, get up and follow me. It's not far." He started up the incline.

Hanna wasn't about to be left. They were walking an overgrown path, branches clawed at her. Her lungs exploded with a sudden fit of coughing, she bent and tried to stifle the sound with her hands.

Clete turned around. "You're doing fine. You can make it, we're almost there."

Hanna squinted and saw a square, dark shape a few yards ahead. She began to move again. He kept a steadying arm around her waist. The shape was a wooden shed. Clete pushed the door open.

It was pitch-black inside. They were standing on a spongy, uneven surface, the air smelled of rotted hay. Clete switched on a flashlight, revealing a backpack in the straw. He took out a quilted nylon jacket. Bracing the light so the beam was on Hanna, he stuffed her into the coat, zipped it, and pulled her into his arms.

"How do you feel? Your face is bruised and you have a cut on your lip. Are you hurt anywhere else?"

She clung to him. "I don't think so. My arms and wrists, a little. I was so damned scared. How did you find the chalet?"

"Easy." He brushed her hair back and kissed her temple, his lips brushed her cheek, then he pushed her away. "Hanna, a lot of things have to be cleared up between us, but not now, baby. There isn't time. Sit back and pay attention.

"I've scouted the house. I saw Frank in a bedroom upstairs, through a balcony window. He's tied to a chair, and he's unconscious. Octavian, Jackie, and the Hippo have been working on him.

"There's another guy tramping around out front. Is that the lot? Besides Madame Mercier in the kitchen?"

Hanna considered. "Yes . . . No. I almost forgot Cici."

"Who's Cici?"

"Helene's maid. That's how they found us, they kidnapped Cici and forced her to bring them here."

"Then she's on our side. Do you know where she is? Tied up somewhere?"

"I don't know. You can't count on her to help us, either, she's too damn terrified. When Octavian and Jackie left the kitchen the first time they didn't tie her up. Octavian told her to fix some food and make tea. Frank was still downstairs then. He talked to her, so did I. She wouldn't listen. She thinks they won't hurt her if she does what she's told."

"Has she turned completely? If she sees something going down, will she tell them?"

"I don't know, she might. You didn't see her in the room with them?"

"No."

Clete was thinking about what she'd told him. "Wait a minute. They went up once, leaving Frank with you, then came back and got him? What's the attraction upstairs?"

"The telephone. There's an extension in the master bedroom. The other one was in the kitchen, they ripped it out of the wall."

"I saw it. Do you have any idea who they're telephoning?"

"Octavian told Jackie he was going to send for a helicopter from 'across the border' to pick them up at dawn. There's a landing pad here, behind the parking area."

"A helicopter! Ah, hell, that puts a different light on things. I saw the wind sock, but it didn't register. Who would expect a heliport here? Octavian couldn't have known, either. Lucky bastard."

He talked on, thinking aloud. "The weather stinks, but it could clear enough for a chopper to get in by morning. You said dawn?"

"That's what he told Jackie. I didn't hear the actual phone call, they were upstairs."

"So he plans to clear out. Does he have the triptych?"

"No. At least, not yet. It's in the chalet. We'd just taken it out of the box when they started pounding on the door. Helene went to answer, but I knew something was wrong. Guests, in this weather?

"We were in the kitchen, the triptych had been stuffed away in a cabinet for forty years. When Helene left the room I hid it, but it won't be hard to find. There was no time!"

"You did well to conceal it at all. If you hadn't, you'd all have been dead before I got here. You bought us some time, Hanna, I'm proud of you."

"Clete, Frank told me Madeleine Anderson's will left the triptych to her church, and that you and he were hired to bring it back."

Hurt feelings piled on top of indignation. "You thought I knew about the triptych and was going to steal it. You rat. You bastard. I didn't even find out Madeleine was dead until I tried to contact her after I was already here.

"As for the triptych, I didn't know it existed. Why couldn't you have said something, instead of jumping to conclusions. . . ."

Clete interrupted, "We don't have time to thrash this out, Hanna. It won't matter, if we don't get out of here. Come on, we've got a lot to do."

He turned off the flashlight and walked outside. Hanna followed, still angry.

"Why did we come up here, anyway? It was a waste of time, we should have been on our way to get help. I could have rested in the car, told you everything I know on the way back to Langenbruck."

"We aren't going to Langenbruck, there isn't time. Do you have any idea how long it would take to get down the mountain, find the local authorities and persuade them to help, then get back up here? We wouldn't have dared risk it anyway, but things are worse than I thought, with this helicopter business.

"You have to go back inside and stay put until I come for you. Pray no one's missed you."

She grabbed his arm. "You can't expect me to do that!"

Clete pulled her against him. She was rigid with anger and fear. He spoke softly.

"Listen, Hanna, I know how you feel, but there's one of me and four of them. It's three o'clock in the morning, it'll be daylight in four hours. Give me a few minutes to work something out now that I know the setup. Okay?"

Hanna pushed his arms away and turned her back. She couldn't talk, so she shrugged and started walking.

Clete caught up with her. "You'll be okay, Frank's fading the heat right now. I'll be back before you know it."

Hanna didn't answer. She slapped a branch away from her face and walked faster.

T·W·E·N·T·Y-F·I·V·E

CLETE dropped from the window ledge and stood splayed against the wall, protected from the upstairs windows by the balcony.

He had to get back to the Saab. He was tempted to sprint across the road in front of the chalet. To work his way uphill, cross over, and then descend on the other side was safer, but time-consuming. Access downhill from the rear was blocked by a granite bluff.

His white clothes were camouflage in the snow, and the man out front wasn't hunting trouble. He decided to chance it. A deep breath and he broke into a run, head down, body low to the ground.

He heard a shout and accelerated, ending up spread-eagle behind a spruce tree. He rolled over and reached for the Beretta in a single movement.

Nothing happened. Whatever the disturbance, it must have been inside the house.

On the downhill slope he thought about Hanna. Her absence

hadn't been noticed. No one was waiting for them, no alarm raised.

A miracle, since Octavian didn't have the triptych. It wouldn't be long before they finished off Frank and started on her. They had to have the triptych before dawn.

The front-yard watchman was whistling as he passed, four bars, endlessly repeated. Making noise to keep himself awake. Clete picked up speed, leaving the chalet behind him.

Octavian, Jackie, Hippo, and the outside watchman. Four of them.

Would he get any help at all? Frank might be hurt bad, the Mercier woman was in a coma, maybe dead. The maid was dangerous.

That left Hanna. She might hate him but she'd do what was necessary. Hadn't even complained when he stripped off the borrowed jacket before he tied her back in the chair.

Nervous sweat made his skin clammy under the layers of clothing. He forced himself to stop and sit on a boulder. Dropping the backpack, he took a granola bar from a zippered compartment, pulled off his ski mask and ate. As he munched, the beginnings of a plan formed in his mind.

He wiped away crumbs, stuffed the wrapper in his pocket, and ran the last few hundred yards, rehearsing. A go-for-broke deal, but it could work.

He unlocked the trunk and lifted out a full five-liter gas can; with a little rummaging he found the tire tool, then shut the trunk and started uphill in an easy lope, buoyed by a rush of optimism.

The wind sock at the helipad creaked in protest as gusts bellied it from north to east. Lying in the snow, Clete spotted the four light posts that formed perimeter boundaries.

He crawled to a spot in the center of the pad and began loosening snow and dirt with the tire tool. Not as difficult as he had expected, the earth wasn't frozen solid. He scooped out the hole as he went. The tool hit solid rock with a metallic chunk at the eighteen-inch level.

He felt with a gloved hand and satisfied himself the hole was deep enough, then scooped out the remaining dirt and returned to the edge of the helipad for the gas can.

Crawling awkwardly with the can clutched to his middle, he went back to the hole. He gave the lid a twist to jam it tight and eased the can in, broad side up. When the metal was covered to his satisfaction he smoothed the churned area. Falling snow would do the rest of the job.

The guard was now slumped on the top step, head lolling. Clete moved in closer. The man's Uzi had fallen from his slack fingers.

I could take him, easy.

No. The plan's made, stick with it.

He went to the parking area and squatted between the two cars.

First the BMW. Let it be unlocked.

It was. He tripped the latch and reached inside, feeling for the hood trigger.

"Ah, gotcha." He tripped it, there was a screech-bang as the lever released and the hood popped.

They must have heard it.

They hadn't. He became more confident; if noises penetrated the chalet walls they'd figure it was their own man moving around. Not much danger of discovery at this point, with the scumbag around in front dead to the world.

He lifted the hood and pulled a wire loose to disable the ignition.

His cheek itched under the mask. He rubbed it and squatted beside the Mercedes. He couldn't keep from looking at the second-floor window. No one was visible in the oblong of yellow light.

It was easy to disable the Mercedes and cut the horn wire. He held the severed ends between thumb and forefinger, his free hand groped the battery. He hesitated.

Once the hot wire made contact all hell would break loose. If things worked out the way he planned, he could do it. If not . . . ?

Another few seconds and he'd talk himself into the shakes. He closed his eyes and jammed the wire against the battery. The horn began to wail.

T·W·E·N·T·Y-S·I·X

SOME bastard was ripping off strips of canvas. The sound infuriated Frank—no one could sleep with that racket.

Holy Mother, he must've tied one on. His gut was on fire; his body felt like an abandoned hand puppet.

Someone was jabbering. He could hear excited voices above the tearing canvas.

He wasn't in bed. He was in Switzerland, in a chalet. About to die. Octavian Demopolis was expounding on something, Hippo and LeBeau joining in on cue like a Greek Chorus.

Frank's tailbone was poking a hole in the chair. He had to move.

If they caught him they'd know he was conscious. It would start again.

"Where is Clete Cross?" Bam.

"Where's Cross?" Bam.

"Where is he?" Bam.

The canvas ripped when he inhaled.

No, that wasn't exactly it. More like bubbling water.

Or a lung punctured by a shattered rib. Shit.

He was getting too old for this kind of thing, couldn't stay awake for thirty-six hours like he used to. Climbed into the Peugeot for a ten-minute rest, and was dead to the world. Next thing he knew Hippo was hauling his butt out of the car and baying like a hound at the kill.

Clete would find them.

Yeah, what was left of them.

Suddenly the voices became more than a leitmotif. They'd found the triptych. He thought about Hanna and began to listen in earnest. Had they already killed her?

"Good work, Jackie, excellent. Up to your old standards. You found it for yourself, without a word from Anders?"

Jackie was burbling with self-pride. "No need. Caught my foot on something in that damn little dark passage under the stairs, a piece of cloth, like what we tied 'em up with. Seemed odd to me, so I took it into the kitchen and had a good look. There was soot on it, then I saw soot on the floor all around the fireplace and took a closer look. The triptych was inside some kind of iron oven deal built into the fireplace. They damn near roasted this baby!"

"Barbarians!" Real emotion in Octavian's voice.

"Big Red almost choked, she thought I was going to off her right then. I told her not a chance, not 'til Hippo and I finish with her." In the sudden chill silence, Jackie saw fit to amend his words. "I mean—"

"Never mind what you mean."

So Hanna was still alive. Frank moved restlessly, testing the linen strips that bound him. They were too occupied with the triptych to notice if he stripped naked and did the hula with an American flag between his teeth.

Not that he was capable of much if he did get loose, but he couldn't sit trussed like a pig in a slaughterhouse.

Octavian was talking about Hanna. The incident in Geneva. LeBeau interrupted, so charged up he was almost incoherent.

"Hell of it is, I believe her. She didn't know you from the

Pope's Prime Minister. What a piece of mother luck. Interesting face!

"She was her own damn Judas goat. Led us straight to this baby. Kismet. Goddamn, bloody fate. What do you figure it's worth?"

"That is not a matter for speculation. More than money. More than anybody's life, if it's mentioned after tonight. The triptych is mine."

Crazy sonofabitch. He'd wipe out half a continent to get a bauble. Won't lose an eyelash over killing four people, but one scratch on his play-pretty'd send him into shock.

Clete's not going to make it. I'm going to die here.

For some reason he thought of his eighth-grade teacher at Ascención del Cristo. Sister Stanislaus. Fat, cheerful German nun in a school full of Latinos. Kids called her Sister Santa Claus.

She made Frank Rivera feel special, like maybe he could break away, escape the legacy of a family that already had two sons doing time in the joint.

Well, here I am, Sister. Foreign travel, excitement. Just like you said.

What the hell was that!

A car horn, caterwauling like a flick of the bone in Octavian's face!

Clete, you sweet sonofabitch, what are you up to?

A bloody smile creased Frank's face, exposing a newly chipped tooth.

T·W·E·N·T·Y-S·E·V·E·N

JACKIE'S visit, his discovery of the triptych, had sent Hanna spiraling into mindless panic. She tried to force herself to recite. Anything. The Gettysburg Address, the Twenty-third Psalm.

All she could remember was a jumble of Poe.

> The raven still is sitting
> Never flitting
> Never flitting . . .
> Just above my chamber door
> And his eyes have all the seeming
> of a demon's that is dreaming . . .
> Nevermore
> Nevermore.

Someone screamed, her insides convulsed.

No, a car horn.

Impossible.

Jackie shouted from upstairs. "Dieter? Dieter, what the hell's going on?"

The horn stopped. Spurts of profanity were punctuated by heavy footfalls down the stairs. Hippolyte stuck his head in, checked the room, disappeared. The front door slammed.

"Dieter, goddammit, Octavian wants to know what you're doing!" Jackie, shouting from upstairs again.

"Hanna? What is it . . ." Helene! Sounding groggy but lucid. She even remembered to speak English.

"Oh, God, Helene, I thought you were in a coma, dying. How are you? I mean, I know you feel like hell, but are you okay? Is anything broken? You were unconscious so long."

"My head hurts. I do not see well. But I do not . . . think . . . I have broken bones."

"Keep your head still, you might have a concussion. Flex your fingers and wrists, if you can. It'll hurt, but you need to keep the blood circulating in your arms and hands."

"Yes, I will do that. Did I hear shouting? Those men are still here? Where is Cici?"

"Two of the men are upstairs, they have Frank Rivera and Cici. The others are outside. There was some kind of disturbance."

"What happened to me? I cannot seem to remember."

"Octavian hit you. You passed out, I thought your neck was broken."

"Passed out? Oh, I see. Well, it does not seem to be. What did you say is happening outside?"

"I don't know. A car horn blaring, men shouting. Let's listen." Helene nodded.

Hanna wanted to tell her about Clete. It could wait, there was so much to explain. She expected to hear Hippolyte come back, bringing a rueful and apologetic Dieter along. Maybe she could overhear something.

Minutes dragged by. She was confused. Had she missed them while she talked to Helene?

"Hippo? Have you found Dieter?" Jackie, yelling from the window again.

"Dieter? One of you better get up here and do some explaining!"

With a sharp, brittle eruption glass imploded into the kitchen; flying shards sprayed across the room. Helene screamed.

A figure catapulted inside. Clete.

He slashed Hanna free and shoved her toward the window.

"Did you get help?" she asked over her shoulder.

"Out!" He crowded behind her, carrying Helene.

Hanna scrabbled through, landed on her feet and ran across the parking area into sheltering trees. Furious shouts came from upstairs, punctuated by fire from an automatic weapon.

Clete pushed past. "Come on, Hanna, up to the shed."

The guns stuttered again. Hanna panicked, her knees were jelly. She crawled, pulled herself along uneven ground.

"Wait, please. I'm coming. Don't leave me behind."

She staggered into an uneven lope.

Where the path steepened she stumbled on a rock and fell. Pain stabbed the injured knee, she felt along the bone and pulled out a sliver of glass.

Clete was out of sight now. Was someone behind her? She lurched up and crashed through branches like a wounded animal until she came to the clearing in front of the shed.

Clete waited with Helene in his arms. He saw Hanna and kicked the door open. She staggered past and sprawled.

"I . . . can't . . . breathe!"

"Yes, you can. Don't hyperventilate, damn it, take it easy. Steady, steady, control your breaths. You can do it. We're safe for a while."

"Sure," Hanna gasped.

"No, we really are. They won't follow, at least not right away. They don't know what's out here." He switched on a flashlight and propped it up.

Helene lay where he'd put her, unconscious again. Clete

straightened her arms and legs and pulled the full skirt down, tucking it around her boots.

Hanna crawled over and sat beside them.

"She came around for a few minutes, before you scared the wits out of her. She was rational. What do you think it is, a concussion?"

"You told me Octavian slapped her around? I hope a concussion's all that's wrong; she looks pretty fragile. If she talked and made sense, it's a good sign."

"Tell me what happened. Where are Dieter and Hippolyte?"

"I wired the Mercedes' horn. The guy in front . . . Dieter? . . . He must be a new hand, I haven't run across him before.

"Anyway, he came and stuck his head under the hood, right on cue. I damn near decapitated him.

"Then Hippo showed up, bitching so loud he wouldn't have noticed me if I yodeled like Tarzan and beat my chest.

"I took him from behind. Real pleasure, I must say. Dragged him by the heels and stuffed him in the Mercedes with his friend. Then I came for you."

"Are they dead?"

"I hope so."

"What will Octavian do? Come after us? Kill Frank and Cici? Or both?"

"They're not going to kill anybody right now, they need hostages to shield their getaway.

"I don't believe they'll come after us either, since they don't have any idea how many people are out here. We could have a dozen armed men."

"I wish."

"Bluff's everything right now, Hanna. They're going to stay safe inside as long as they can."

Hanna wished he didn't sound like a boy whistling his way through the graveyard.

He reached for her hand and put something in it. A flask.

"You're shaking. Have some of that while I get you a jacket. Go easy, it'll blow your head off."

"Don't tell me, let me guess. Brandy." She sipped, in seconds the alcohol was in her bloodstream. She wiped her mouth and handed back the flask.

"Then it's a standoff? We can't just hole up here and let them take off in the helicopter."

"Right. We're going inside, one more time."

Not this half of we. He can't expect that, damn it. Not to help Cici, not even to save his friend Frank. I can't do it. I won't.

"Can you shoot?"

"What? Oh. I'm pretty good with a shotgun, I used to shoot skeet with Dad. I fired a pistol in college during a self-defense course. Never got to be expert at it, so don't expect too much."

"What kind of pistol?"

"Old .44 caliber I borrowed from a neighbor. He called it a 'Cattle Rustler's Special.'"

"Then maybe you can manage this, if you have to." He laid something heavy in her lap. She scooted closer to the light.

"Careful with that, damn it. I thought you'd handled guns before."

"Oh, come on. What is this thing?"

"An Uzi. Automatic, fires twenty-five rounds without reloading. You just pull the trigger and hang on."

"Clete, I'm not sure . . ."

"Neither am I. I hope we won't have to find out." He reached for the gun.

"Take the light and watch me a minute."

She swung the flashlight at him.

"Not in my eyes! Look at my hands. This is the way you hold it, I have the stock bolted on for you. Brace yourself, it jumps. You might end up shooting at the sky."

"Sounds dangerous in the hands of an amateur."

"It is. I took it off Dieter. There's nothing else available. My

Beretta's more your size, but I'll be working in close quarters. The Uzi would be awkward.

"Now. You have to squeeze to fire, like this. Not just pull the trigger. Built-in safety feature.

"Don't be tempted to play sharpshooter. If there's a friendly body within fifty feet of your target aim above their heads. You'll scare hell out of 'em, at least."

"I hear that. Scared hell out of me, when Octavian and Jackie were shooting at us."

"Look Hanna, this is a selector switch. I'm setting it to limit firing to three-round bursts. Let up on the trigger, squeeze again, and you get three more. Understand?"

"You mean, so I won't go berserk and keep shooting until I've blown away everything on the mountain? Good precaution. Women can't be trusted to have good sense."

"Don't be so damn touchy. You're not used to the thing, is all. The safety's on. I'll take it off for you when we get inside."

"We might as well settle this now, Clete. . . ."

"Be careful! Don't get straw in the mechanism, you'll cause a misfire."

"Clete, I'm not going in that place again."

"Yes, you are. Listen to me. I mean to get Frank out of there, and the damn girl, if I can find her. You're going to create a diversion.

"Here's how it goes. They're not about to leave the bedroom unless something forces them out. They have to figure they've lost the expendables, Hippo and Dieter. Why risk exposing their own precious carcasses until they have to?"

"Get to the part where I create a diversion."

"I'll scout the place first. If the downstairs is clear, we'll go back in together. We'll take that cloth I saw on the kitchen table and plant you at the bottom of the stairs with it.

"I have lighter fluid. We'll douse the fabric, I'll leave, you wait five minutes. If Octavian or LeBeau come down, blast away. Make damn sure they're not using Frank as a shield before you do."

"What if they are? Do I throw up my hands and say, 'You win'?"

"You shoot above their heads, throw a match on the cloth, and run like hell. But that won't happen.

"Now. Here's how it will go. When five minutes are up, light the fire. Make sure it's burning well, slip out the front door, and come up here. Run. Don't look back and don't stop, no matter what you hear. Got it?"

"What will you be doing? I don't want to hog all the good stuff."

"I'll be up on the balcony. When they smell smoke they'll have to investigate, they're not about to sit up there and be roasted alive. And they're not the type to save prisoners, they'll abandon Frank and the girl.

"If they realize it's no big deal, I expect they'll put it out and stay inside. Meanwhile I'll have hijacked the prisoners."

"What if you can't get in? What if only one of them leaves, or they come onto the balcony themselves? What if you can't get Frank and Cici out, and the chalet burns?"

Clete didn't answer.

"Clete?"

"We've got to risk it. Don't think the things you mentioned haven't occurred to me, plus a few more. I've tried to come up with a better plan. I can't."

She heard him moving around in the dark, a weight fell on her shoulders. She reached up, touched the jacket, and slipped into it.

"Sorry. I damn near forgot to give it to you. Why didn't you say something?"

"I was going to. Tell the truth, I didn't need it. Thanks to your firewater, and the thrill of hearing you describe what you expect me to do."

She made slow work fastening the jacket. She knew he was waiting for an answer.

She made up her mind. "If you say that's our best shot, let's get on with it."

He squeezed her shoulder. "I did consider waiting until the helicopter comes, but that's riskier. They might figure they don't need both hostages, chances are they'd kill one inside the chalet. The other would be shot as soon as they're safe."

"I'm ready." Hanna picked up the Uzi.

Helene stirred and began to cough.

"Clete, what about her? She must be freezing, that won't help her condition. Let me put this jacket on her. My coat is on a chair in the house, we can get it."

Clete stopped her. "Keep it, you won't be any good to me if you're numb with cold. There're blankets in my car, I'll go for them when I can. Until then we can pull straw over her body. It'll insulate as well as anything if she doesn't move too much. Hurry."

They scooped straw and piled it on, until only Helene's face was uncovered.

"Know what this reminds me of?" Hanna asked. "The beach, covering someone with sand.

"I hope she doesn't wake while we're gone. She'd be terrified. Alone in the dark, with no idea where she is or what's happened."

"We've gone to the trouble of covering her, and she's not bound. That should be some reassurance. We've done the best we can. Are you ready now?"

"Yes."

"Wait. How long since you've eaten? In Langenbruck? Better try this." He handed her a granola bar.

"Go on, eat it. You need the energy."

Hanna took a bite and began to chew. Her mouth was dry, it was like trying to swallow ground cement.

"Let's go. I'll eat it on the way."

Clete switched off the flashlight. They stood outside the door, letting their eyes adjust to the night.

"Clete, I want to say something. Hear me out, it won't take a minute.

"I told you Frank filled me in about Madeleine's will, and you two being hired by the Church to bring back the triptych.

"Why couldn't you have told me that? I've been as scared of you as I was of Jackie and the others. I'm not completely stupid, you know. Your story about being a banker stunk.

"I'm going to tell you this once more. If you don't believe me . . ." She shrugged. "Then you don't.

"I didn't know Madeleine was dead. I didn't know there was a Fabergé triptych. I don't want it if it's not mine.

"What harm would it have done to assume I was honest and tell me the truth?"

"I don't know, Hanna, there's no simple answer. I was tempted to trust you, but it seemed too much of a coincidence, you showing up right after she died.

"I'd seen Octavian run after you in Geneva, then try to kidnap you in Basel. It was obvious he thought you were the key to the triptych."

"I suppose I was, without realizing it."

• • •

Clete couldn't think of anything else to say. Maybe she expected an apology; he wasn't ready to make one.

They were halfway down the path. He yawned and looked up at the sky. A high full moon made fleeting appearances between fast-moving clouds. The front was breaking up.

Hanna had her back to him; she seemed nervous, making swipes at the snow with the toe of her boot as she walked. Her long hair fell loose around her shoulders, dark against the white nylon jacket.

"Better cover your hair with the hood, you'll be less visible in the snow. Here, I'll help you."

He gathered the silky mass and tucked it in, pulled the hood strings, and tied them under her chin. They moved on.

Long, tumbled hair, dark against the white coat, reminded him of something. Another young woman; tall and slim, with long, loose hair.

His mother, tears streaming down her face. Cursing, crying. Stalking up and down a room too small to hold her.

Himself, ten years old, begging to be told what was wrong.

"They murdered him, the bastards. John Kennedy is dead, his brains spattered all over Dallas." She screamed at him. "They've killed the President."

Clete was terrified. It wasn't possible. The President was real, not just a face on the TV. Clete's parents talked about John Kennedy like he was family.

Clete tried to think of a way to comfort his mother. All he could say was, "Call Daddy. Please call Daddy. He'll know what to do."

Clete's foot twisted on a rock, he grabbed a tree branch to steady his descent.

His mother hadn't been the same after Kennedy's death. When Clete's father died and they moved to Boston, the disintegration accelerated. Liquor and nostalgia, both in excess.

Why on earth had he dredged that up?

Oh. Another woman. Long hair, dark against a light jacket. Hanna, who wavered between independence and vulnerability.

A brittle stick snapped under her foot. She looked back at him and shrugged a silent apology.

Clumsy. Tall, skinny redhead. Why did he let her get under his skin?

Women couldn't stand up under pressure. His mother had seemed strong. Death, changes; she crumpled up like a broken doll.

Oh, women had their uses. Good times. Sweet, lithe bodies.

Long, sensuous legs, wrapped around you in bed. Full breasts; firm, yielding. Pert, pink-tipped nipples. Like Marga.

They came to the bottom of the path. He whispered last instructions and they moved softly toward the chalet.

He was going to have to trust a woman now.

T·W·E·N·T·Y-E·I·G·H·T

HANNA had a coin-sized birthmark behind her right ear that burned like the devil when she was stressed out. She dug at it with a reckless forefinger as she watched Clete sprint across the open space behind the cars.

He made it. No stuttering spray of bullets. No Clete writhing in the snow, mortally wounded.

She could see him silhouetted against the chalet, his white clothing that blended so well in the snow was starkly visible against the dark wall.

He climbed through the kitchen window and disappeared. Her orders were to wait under cover until he came back and gave her the signal to follow.

The birthmark felt like someone had smashed out a cigarette against it. She picked up snow, squeezed it into a pellet, and soothed the spot.

She felt so damned fragile. Bones, flesh, delicate things. She imagined her body mangled and broken, warm blood leaking, dissolving the snow into pink slush.

The cars were between her and the chalet. What if Hippo

wasn't dead? What if he staggered out of the Mercedes and grabbed her, like one of the boogie man figures in a wax museum.

The BMW was only yards away. A few hours ago she and Helene had driven it up the mountain road. Two women in a snappy yellow car, filled with high adventure.

Helene had left the keys in the ignition. Hanna could jump inside, lock the doors, and drive to Langenbruck for help. She could. No one would blame her. No one but Clete.

All Clete cared about was Frank Rivera.

She'd been careful not to look at the upstairs window. It would have to be done, she couldn't leave the sheltering trees without seeing what might be watching out of that glass rectangle.

She looked. Someone had pulled the curtains, a slender blade of light ran vertically up the middle where they didn't quite meet.

Movement caught her attention, a white shape spilled from the kitchen window just below the one she watched; Clete stood and motioned with his right arm.

She didn't acknowledge the signal.

She could make it to Langenbruck in the BMW. The roads were hell, but she was an experienced mountain driver.

No, damn it, she couldn't run.

She turned away from the cars, waved at Clete, and was off in a crouched run, aping his earlier trip. On the last stride she slipped and skidded into him, they fell together in dead flowers, enmeshed in a hostile embrace.

Disentanglement of arms and legs was a slow pantomime, executed with the precision of a pair of street mimes. When he was free Clete dropped to one knee, raising the other to make a footrest. He pointed to the window and took the Uzi from her.

Hanna stepped up, braced both hands on the sill, and crawled inside. The kitchen light was still on, she squinted against the glare and dropped to the floor. She was so frightened it took terrible concentration to control the movements of her body.

Clete came through, carrying the Uzi for her. He motioned

toward the inside door. She crossed the room, wincing at the crunch of glass shards from the broken windowpane.

He was beside her, one arm loaded with linens, the other holding the Uzi and her sheepskin coat that he'd retrieved from the sitting room. She took the coat and put it on, he handed her the Uzi.

It was dark in the dining room. Clete found her free hand and put it on his shoulder. They blind marched through the small chamber under the stairs into the main room. Light from the windows made it possible to see outlines of furniture, a few rosy embers glowed in the fireplace.

At the staircase he squatted and motioned her to sit. He dumped the linens just below the bottom step and drenched them with lighter fluid. Fumes stung Hanna's nose, she pushed a finger against her upper lip to stifle a sneeze.

Clete reached for her hand and put five large kitchen matches in her palm. She felt his lips against her ear.

"Five minutes. Three hundred seconds, count them off. Light a match and throw it, don't get too close. When you're sure it's burning, get out. Don't stop until you get to the shed. I mean it, Hanna. Don't stop. I can't worry about you. Is that clear?"

She nodded.

"Give me the Uzi, I'll switch off the safety."

When he handed back the gun he surprised her with a brief kiss and was gone.

She didn't care what he said, she wasn't going to that shed until she saw what happened. She could take cover in the trees and wait. Maybe Frank or Cici was badly hurt, if he brought them both out she could help.

And if everything went to hell, if they killed Clete, she needed to know. Not hide in the shed like some dumb beast waiting for slaughter.

Her right arm cradled the Uzi. She squinted up the stairs, there was a faint slice of light at the top landing. Her senses were supercharged, if a mouse scratched in the attic she would hear it.

Part of her mind had been marking off seconds, like muffled drums of a funeral dirge.

274. So many ifs. If Jackie and Octavian came down, leaving Frank and Cici.

279. If Frank and Cici were alive, if Clete could get them away in time.

280. She felt for a rough spot to strike matches, reached out and patted the linen. Still damp with lighter fluid.

296. The triptych. Would Clete bring it out? No, he'd have his hands full with Frank and Cici. The triptych was no longer important to anyone but Octavian.

299. She struck a match and tossed it on the linen, it flashed, settled to blue flame. Brilliant, splendid in darkness, rippling across the cloth.

She clutched the Uzi and stood up, then opened her left hand and dropped the rest of the matches on the pyre. They hissed and flared, curtaining the staircase.

Hanna ran.

From the safety of the trees she watched the chalet. She was breathing hard, from fear more than exertion. Her arms ached from clutching the Uzi. A tree forked invitingly beside her shoulder, she lifted the barrel and rested it.

Clete was on the balcony, a white, motionless figure. Life seemed to be arrested in motion, a stop-action photo of a horse race.

The fire must be belching smoke by now.

With the bedroom door shut they might not smell it in time.

God, please let them smell it.

Clete burst into action, he kicked out the window and disappeared. Hanna gripped the Uzi in its tree-fork rest. She counted seconds again.

Figures appeared in the frame of light. One, two, out on the balcony. Only two.

They were coming down slowly, Clete assisting Frank. It was Frank, she could tell by the size of the figure.

"Hurry, hurry!" she whispered.

Jackie came out the window, howling in fury. Clete and Frank were huddled under the balcony, Jackie leaned over it to fire. Hanna leveled the Uzi in the tree fork, swung it to face the chalet, and stopped to sight up the barrel.

Clete and Frank were trapped.

Clete fired the Beretta. It sounded puny. Impotent, like an air gun. He shot up through the overhang, trying to drive them back inside.

Octavian had come to join Jackie, there were bursts of answering fire from both their weapons.

Hanna steadied the Uzi with her left hand. She squeezed the trigger, aiming high. Her three-round burst went wide to the right and high, but it was effective. Octavian and Jackie scuttled back through the window.

She released the grip and squeezed again. The second three rounds knocked off a chunk of wooden roof.

Clete and Frank had crossed the open area and reached the shelter of the cars. Now they reappeared from behind the Mercedes and entered the trees a few yards away.

"Clete! Here."

"You come here. Don't shoot anymore."

She lifted the Uzi out of the tree. Muscles in her arms jumped.

"Hanna?"

"Coming." She crawled toward his voice, watching the chalet. All upstairs lights were now off. The single kitchen window threw out a beam like a false beacon, luring sailors onto the rocks.

She found the men. "Thanks," was Clete's brief greeting. It was enough.

Hanna looked at Frank. "Are you okay?"

"Hell, no. My ribs are crushed. I think that bastard ruptured my gut. What took you guys so long?"

Clete grinned, shook his head.

"So much for alibis," Frank said. "What's next?"

"There's a shed, quarter of a mile uphill. Hanna's friend is there, hurt and unconscious. Think you can make it?"

"Yeah, if you don't rush me. Where's the little French maid?"

"We thought you'd tell us," Clete said.

"I never saw her again, after she left the kitchen with food for Octavian."

"Do you think they killed her?" Hanna asked. She felt guilty about how furious she'd been with Cici.

Nobody answered. The silence became uncomfortable.

Clete broke it. "There's tape in my backpack. I'll bring it down and bind your ribs. I've got something for pain, too."

Frank shook his head. "No, let's do it up there. I can manage, I'd just as soon put a little more distance between us and them, thank you. Let's get it over with."

Clete stood. "Can I help?"

"No, I'll do better by myself." Frank took hold of a tree limb and pulled up. He swayed and bent over, one arm clamped to his side.

Hanna thought how painful it must have been for him, coming off the balcony. She looked at Clete.

"Lead the way, will you, Hanna?" he said in a bleak voice.

T·W·E·N·T·Y-N·I·N·E

HELENE, we're back. Can you hear me?"

Helene was exactly as they had left her, face up, covered with moldy straw. Her green eyes were slitted open in a vacant stare. Hanna uncovered one of her hands and began to chafe. It felt lifeless, the skin had a bluish tinge. Rosy polish on beautifully manicured nails seemed incongruous flecked with bits of decaying vegetation.

Clete had brought supplies from his car. Hanna picked up a blanket.

Was it better to pull the straw away and wrap Helene, or lay the blanket over straw and all?

She turned to ask Clete.

His head was bent close to Frank's, their lowered voices were taut with suppressed urgency. She decided not to interrupt.

A lantern that had been in the store of things Clete retrieved from his car burned between Hanna and the men. It was the self-contained kind, with a small propane cartridge for fuel. The windows of the shed were boarded up, it didn't seem dangerous to have a light.

Home away from home, all the comforts.

Hanna nibbled a cracker and sipped coffee. Strong, hot heavenly.

She looked at Helene again.

You and I shouldn't be involved in this. A retired school mistress and an artist, we're not very well equipped for deadly games.

Octavian can have the triptych if it means so much to him. Why won't he just take it and go? He doesn't have to kill us.

There's Jackie. He hates me, honest to God hates me. He's a con man and a thief, probably a murderer, but he's furious because I wasn't bowled over by his charm. I actually hurt his feelings. How do people get like that?

I feel like someone who's fallen through the looking glass and ended up in Alice's nightmare.

She looked at Clete and Frank again. Every line of their bodies conveyed dreadful urgency.

Too bad she didn't have a conté crayon and paper. Could she capture that intensity of feeling?

Could anyone?

A great empathy with Clete welled up. What a responsibility they were, looking to him for miracles; two women and his battered friend.

What could he possibly do? Getting the three of them out of the Chalet under Octavian's nose had been feat enough.

That's right, maybe it had been enough. Maybe they just had to wait it out until the helicopter left at daylight, then make their way down the mountain.

It's not that simple. Octavian doesn't play by the rules of sane people, that's what makes him scary.

Maybe he's let us get this far to amuse himself. Any minute the cat will get bored and eat the mouse.

She touched Helene's cheek. "Lucky Helene. Either we'll tell you about this when it's over and you're safe in a hospital somewhere, or you'll never know at all.

Hanna's coffee cup was empty, she set it aside and leaned against the wall. Her eyes closed. Fear couldn't hold back exhaustion forever.

The men's voices buzzed softly, now and then a word or phrase carried.

"Helicopter . . . if the girl is alive . . . How many rounds?"

She was asleep when Clete called.

"Hanna, come here, will you?"

She stretched, walked over, and curled up in her favorite cross-legged position.

Frank turned away and began sorting some things in a small canvas bag, removing himself from the conversation.

Clete began to talk. "Frank and I have a plan. It's after six now, almost daylight, so I don't have time to explain. You'll have to take orders from me one more time."

"Why can't we stay here until they leave in the helicopter? Let them have the triptych, it can't be that important to you."

"Damn it, Hanna, what about the girl?"

"Oh, Clete, I can't believe I forgot Cici."

"It's not just her. Octavian won't leave until we're all dead. From the helicopter they'll be able to spot this shed in a minute; there's no place we could hide for long.

"And to set the record straight, I don't give a damn about the triptych right now."

Hanna had an attack of fatalism. "That's right, Octavian has to kill us. I keep forgetting that."

"He intends to kill us. Frank and I have a surprise for him."

"Clete, there's something I need to tell you, in case you're counting on my help. You might have the idea I'm dependable, even brave, because I went back in the chalet both times you asked, and lit the fire."

"And covered Frank and me when we were in trouble."

"You do have it wrong.

"Remember when you went in first and left me to wait until you signaled?"

"Yes."

"Well, I almost jumped in the BMW and ran. I damn near deserted everyone."

Clete laughed. "That's your horrible confession? Everyone feels like that at times. Scared and desperate to get the hell out, never mind anyone else. Honorable people don't give in. You didn't.

"Incidently, you'd have been in for a shock if you had. I disabled both cars before I rigged the horn on the Mercedes."

Hanna's confession had humiliated her so badly it took a minute for Clete's words to sink in. "You disabled the BMW? I never thought of that. God, what a fool I would have made of myself."

Clete was serious again. He reached for her hands and gripped them.

"There's nothing for you to do this time but keep quiet and watch. I know you'd rather do that than be left in the shed."

"Right. What about Helene?"

"If things work out, we'll have her to a doctor by midmorning. If not . . . ?"

"If not, it won't matter."

"That sums it up." He looked at his watch.

"Time to go. Give me the Uzi, Frank's going to use my gun."

At the sound of his name Frank looked around and lifted a questioning eyebrow.

Clete nodded. "Ready."

One hand against the wall, Frank pulled himself up on his feet. Clete had taped his ribs and given him something for pain, he walked with a little more ease than before.

Hanna gave Clete the Uzi, they followed Frank outside.

Stars shimmered, remote and chaste above the juniper branches. Thin cloud chains made dark bars across the brightening sky. There was no wind.

Perfect conditions for the helicopter.

What was Clete up to? Was it possible he could shoot the chopper down as it landed? But that would leave Octavian and Jackie holed up in the chalet. With Cici.

Clete put an arm around her. "Frank and I are going to position ourselves on the rock ledge above the helipad. I'll find you a place behind us where you can see.

"Hanna, you saved Frank and me back there by disobeying what I told you to do. Don't second guess me this time. Give me your word, no matter what you see and hear, don't move or make a sound. Even if you think everything's gone to hell. Can I count on that?"

"Yes."

"Good. Let's go."

Clete placed her twenty feet behind the lip of the bluff, under a single juniper tree with branches that trailed to the ground. He and Frank crawled to the rim and lay side by side, facing the landing pad.

Hanna wondered which way the chopper would come. Octavian had said "over the border." Which border, German or French?

They'll be coming 'round the mountain when they come. Not driving six white horses, though.

Clete said stay no matter what. Good dog, stay.

Watch Clete die, watch Frank die. Stay under your tree like a faithful pup.

They'll find the shed, drag Helene out, kill her. Here I'll be, under my little tree.

Jackie, crossing the rocks. "I spy. There you are. Come out, Hanna, all's out, 's in free."

Stop it.

The chalet stood out crisp and clean in the gathering light. It looked like the late show on TV; Bing Crosby and Sonia Henie, holding hands and yodeling. Did Bing Crosby ever yodel? She couldn't think.

A vibration. A heartbeat? No. Soft, chuka-chuka-chuka. Rotor blades, beating the air.

Did Clete hear?

He pointed toward a pass between peaks. She followed the line of his arm and saw two pulsing lights. Red, white, red.

Clete and Frank turned their heads in unison to watch the chalet, Hanna looked with them. Nothing moved.

The chopper veered right, then back to skim the side of the mountain. The pilot had found the road from Langenbruck and was following it, coming fast.

She looked at the chalet again and saw the back door move. An arm came out and pointed to the helicopter, then withdrew.

The rotor noise increased. The chopper hovered a few feet above the pad and did a slow rotation.

It was a pretty thing, sleek and white. As she watched, it settled to the ground. The door opened and a black figure jumped out, head down to avoid the whirling blades.

The rotor noise echoed everywhere, it was deafening. Hanna could see plumes of snow kick out in a circle around the craft.

The chalet door burst open and Octavian came out. His left arm held Cici by the throat, his right, a gun. Jackie came behind, carrying the triptych in its box.

"Cici! Fight! Run, baby, run! *À moi, vite!*" Clete shouted at the girl in polyglot French and English.

A miracle happened. Cici dug in her heels and began to struggle.

The man from the helicopter ran to assist Octavian. Frank fired the Beretta, the man jerked into a flopping dance as bullets slammed into his body.

"Let her go, let's get out of here," Jackie screamed.

Octavian shoved Cici to the ground and lunged for the helicopter, Jackie crowded behind him.

"Get away from there, Cici!" Clete yelled.

Cici scrambled toward them on her hands and knees across the snow-blanketed landing pad as the chopper door slammed shut.

A deafening whine echoed across the rock escarpment, the pilot revved his engine and lifted the craft off the ground.

They were going to make it.

"Clete. Clete," Hanna moaned. She wasn't afraid, just overcome by desolate sadness. Whatever he'd intended to do had failed. They'd be hunted down and killed. Clete would die blaming himself.

"You couldn't help it. You tried."

Clete jumped up and fired the Uzi into the ground at the center of the landing pad. A huge orange blossom rose from the earth and caressed the helicopter's belly. Yellow-red petals reached upward, the rotor blades chopped off pieces of fire and flung them outward. The blades themselves followed.

The tormented fuselage twisted and fell with a dull plop, like an aborted firecracker. A round, gray ball of smoke rose and trailed away, spitting debris.

"Oh . . . my . . . God," Hanna whispered.

T·H·I·R·T·Y

"CHRISTIAN, we've been through this over and over, with every possible variation, for the past fifteen minutes."

Hanna shifted the phone impatiently to a new position against her ear.

"I'm sorry I ever told you I was going to meet Clete Cross again."

She listened restively as Christian began to reiterate his list of objections. They seemed to go on forever. She interrupted.

"Stop, please. I know what I'm doing. You're acting like I agreed to meet the Boston Strangler in his hotel room at two o'clock in the morning."

Her voice softened. "Christian, I know you and Malika are worried about me, and I appreciate that. But before I left Basel Clete and I agreed to meet in London on this date, for High Tea at the Brown Hotel. What could be more innocuous?

"Besides, he may not even show up. I haven't heard from him since I left Switzerland.

"That's been . . . what? . . . six weeks? He's probably

gone back to the States, maybe he was just kidding about London."

Christian was ready with a new accusation. Oh, this was really too much. "I do *not* imagine myself to be in love with him, whether or not we met under 'romantic circumstances.'

"Dear heaven, romantic! Hideous, terrifying, are the adjectives that come to mind. I still have nightmares about Jackie LeBeau and Octavian."

She looked at her watch and became crafty. "Christian, what if I call you tonight; say, ten o'clock, London time? I promise. I'll tell you everything that happened."

It worked. She dressed quickly and stood in front of the long mirror on the bathroom door. She studied her reflected image dispassionately, like looking at a portrait model.

What she saw was a slim, elongated figure in a white wool dress, with rounded neck and tight sleeves that puffed at the shoulders. The Ibiza tan was completely gone, her skin was barely darker than the dress.

Her hair was loose, in the damp London air it had life of its own, twisting and curling to just below her shoulders. Against the pale shin and dress it flaunted a riot of color, gold, copper, russet, with hints of violet in the shadows. Her eyes seemed darker, too.

On the middle finger of her right hand she wore the ring Dedushka had given her, on her neck was a gold chain bearing another Ceylon sapphire, circled by small diamonds.

She had bought the dress and necklace in Harrod's the week before, braving throngs of holiday shoppers, feeling a little foolish for spending so much money.

"I won't be disappointed if he's not there," she reassured herself.

She thought about the day she left Basel. Clete had taken her to the train. They talked about Helene, and Frank, and Cici, and how nice the weather had turned, while they loaded her gear into an empty compartment.

"Hanna, I won't be able to leave here for some time. There are things to be thrashed out with the Swiss authorities. Six people dead, a helicopter shot down. I talked them into letting you go because you have a squeaky clean background.

"But me . . . Octavian and I go back a long way. They intend to do a lot of checking before they take my word and Frank's for what happened up there. I don't blame them."

"So?"

"So how long are you going to be in London?"

"Until spring, at least."

"Okay, here's what we'll do. I'll meet you, Sunday before Christmas, for High Tea at the Brown Hotel. You make the reservations. Okay?"

"Clete, that's such a long time. Are you sure . . . all right, I'll be there."

He kissed her, stroked her hair, touched the healing scar on her lip where Octavian had hit her.

"See you then." He was gone before she had time to answer.

He hadn't asked where she was staying. He could have found out from Helene, if he wanted to. Days spun into weeks, she gave up any expectation of hearing from him.

But still there was this, a firm date at a firm time in a designated place. She intended to be there.

She stopped at the desk on her way out to check for mail. There was a letter from Helene, she put it in her purse to read later.

The Brown Hotel wasn't large. Something of an insider's place, warm and cozy. Genuine charm, not the self-conscious glory of more elaborate places.

She moved forward with the line of people waiting to be seated and gave her name to the man checking reservations.

"Anders, Hanna Anders. The reservation is for two, I'm expecting Mr. Clete Cross."

He consulted his list and smiled. "Yes, of course. This way, Miss Anders."

She was seated on a plump little sofa against the wall, behind a low table. "Someone will be with you in a moment."

Hanna looked around the room with approval. Patterned wallpaper, a fireplace with a collection of china dogs, gleaming silver and pink-flowered china on the tables. Nice.

Clete wasn't going to come. He hadn't been serious, had facetiously suggested a meeting as a graceful way to part, better than a flat, final good-bye.

"Will you be having tea alone, ma'am?" A round, pink waitress with a friendly gap-toothed smile.

"I'm . . . sort of expecting someone. I'll wait a little longer, if you don't mind."

"Then I'll bring you a pot of tea now, and serve the food when your friend comes."

"Thank you, I'd appreciate that."

Hanna opened her purse and took out the letter. She slit the envelope with a fingernail and removed two sheets of stationery covered with Helene's beautiful script.

My Dear Hanna,

You must not worry about my health. I get stronger day by day, although I still have headaches, and once in a while bad dreams.

The holiday season is quite festive here. I am beginning to go out a little, and seem to be something of a celebrity. Everyone wants a firsthand account of the events at the chalet.

Do you know, I think talking about it is good for me. Each time I tell the story it becomes less real, as though it were something I read in a book, or saw in a moving picture.

Jules and Clothilde send holiday greetings and their best wishes. Poor Jules, I have had a terrible time convincing him that he was not to blame for Cici's abduction, because he was asleep when those horrible men came.

Clothilde was in the kitchen. By the time she decided

something was wrong and awakened Jules it was too late, the men had gone and taken Cici with them.

Little Cici is recovering faster than I ever expected. She has told me all about the final moments, and is very proud of herself for having the courage to break away from Octavian when Clete Cross commanded her. The American boyfriend tells her she is a heroine.

You have not asked about Clete. I have become acquainted with him in the past weeks; he has formed the habit of visiting me daily since my return from the hospital. Our Swiss authorities have been reluctant to release him, although they did allow Frank Rivera to return to the United States a few days ago.

Clete is a man of substance and worth, Hanna. I like him.

Did I tell you I plan to sell the chalet? It was a hard decision, but I don't think I could ever enjoy visiting there again.

Hanna, I wish you were here, to spend Christmas with us. I worry about you, alone in London. If you should change your mind, come, you will be very welcome.

I look forward to your presence, or at least a letter from you.

Helene

Hanna let the pages fall in her lap. Helene had said the happenings at the chalet seemed like some lurid form of fiction. She felt that too, maybe it was the mind's way of dealing with events too atrocious to contemplate.

The waitress came back. "Miss Anders? You have a telephone call, will you please come with me?"

Hanna followed, feeling disappointment and relief. Clete wasn't coming, but at least he had the courtesy to telephone.

She picked up the receiver at the reservations counter.

"Hello?"

Silence.

"Hello? This is Hanna Anders."

There was no one on the line, maybe he'd been cut off. She

went back to her table, determined not to show disappointment. She would ask the waitress to bring the rest of her tea immediately. Or better, just pay and leave.

There was a package on the table, wrapped in pink paper and tied with a scrap of green silk ribbon. Someone must have made a mistake. She picked it up to look for a card.

Nothing. An added irritation, she'd have to ask the waitress to make inquiries.

"Excuse me, please. I couldn't help seeing you're alone."

Hanna looked up, ready with a scathing reply.

An elderly man stood by the table. He had curly white hair, a neat mustache, and a small, clipped beard. His grooming and erect stance suggested a military background.

"Please forgive an old man for being forward, but I've lost my family for the day. Off visiting relatives. I hate to eat alone, do you suppose we could have tea together?"

Hanna shrugged. "Sit down, if you like. My friend has been . . . detained."

He sat beside her on the sofa and rested his elbow on the lace-doilied arm.

"Looks as if he's sent you a holiday package. Don't mind me, go ahead and open it."

"I can't, it isn't for me. Someone left it by mistake while I was away from the table. There's no card. I was just going to give it to the waitress."

He leaned forward. "If there's no card, how will she know what to do with it? I say open it, maybe there's some identification inside."

He was right. Someone would have to open it, and it had been left at her table. Why not?

She pulled loose the green ribbon and tore into the paper. Inside was a dark green velvet box. No card, no identifying logo. She lifted the lid.

Resting on a bed of velvet were several brilliant colored stones, and three or four that sparkled translucently with every color, reflecting light from the wall sconce behind her. They looked very familiar.

"He must have been here. Clete Cross, my friend. . . ." She began an explanation to the old man.

Only he wasn't an old man. Clete smiled at her, a pile of false hair rested on the table in front of him.

"They're yours, Hanna. They were lying on the bed when I went in after Frank. I couldn't bring the triptych, but I stuffed these in my pocket."

Hanna caught her breath, laughed, babbled. "Clete. You devil! Oh, this is ridiculous. A false beard and mustache. And I fell for it.

"These stones. You had them all the time, and never told me. What if I hadn't taken you seriously, hadn't met you here?"

Clete grinned. "That would have been your tough luck, wouldn't it?"